T5-ANT-783

Praise for

MARILYN PAPPANO

"A good mystery combines with a great romance
for a fantastic book."
—*RT Book Reviews* on *Protector's Temptation*

"Pappano's highly entertaining story has it all.... Once
you start it, you'll be reading until all is revealed."
—*RT Book Reviews* on *Criminal Deception*

"This engrossing, atmospheric story is loaded with
hot, sultry passion and complex characters."
—*RT Book Reviews* on *Scandal in Copper Lake*

Praise for

LINDA CONRAD

"A great romance and adventure that the reader won't
be able to put down."
—*RT Book Reviews* on *The Sheikh's Lost Princess*

"Conrad casts her own magical spell with a terrific
mix of good versus evil and plenty of passion and
sensuality. Readers will be bewitched!"
—*RT Book Reviews* on *In Safe Hands*

"Packed with sincere emotions and realistic danger,
resulting in an intensely satisfying romance."
—*Cataromance.com* on *Safe by His Side*

MARILYN PAPPANO

has spent most of her life growing into the person she was meant to be, but isn't there yet. She's been blessed by family—her husband, their son, his lovely wife and a grandson who is almost certainly the most beautiful and talented baby in the world—and friends, along with a writing career that's made her one of the luckiest people around. Her passions, besides those already listed, include the pack of wild dogs who make their home in her house, fighting the good fight against the weeds that make up her yard, killing the creepy-crawlies that slither out of those weeds and, of course, anything having to do with books.

LINDA CONRAD

When asked about her favorite things, Linda Conrad lists a longtime love affair with her husband, her sweetheart of a dog named KiKi and a sunny afternoon with nothing to do but read a good book. Inspired by generations of storytellers in her family and pleased to have many happy readers' comments, Linda continues creating her own sensuous and suspenseful stories about compelling characters finding love.

A bestselling author of more than twenty-five books, Linda has received numerous industry awards, among them the National Reader's Choice Award, the Maggie, the Write Touch Readers' Award and the *RT Book Reviews* Reviewers' Choice Award. To contact Linda, to read more about her books or to sign up for her newsletter and/or contests, go to her website, www.lindaconrad.com.

MARILYN PAPPANO
LINDA CONRAD

Christmas Confidential

HARLEQUIN®

entertain, enrich, inspire™

ISBN-13: 978-0-373-27801-5

Recycling programs
for this product may
not exist in your area.

CHRISTMAS CONFIDENTIAL

CONTENTS

Dear Reader,

We have exciting news for you! Starting in January, Harlequin Romantic Suspense is unveiling a brand-new look that's a fresh take on our beautiful covers. Turn to the back of the book for a sneak peek.

There's more! Along with new covers, the stories will be longer—more action, more excitement, more romance. Follow your beloved characters on their passion-filled adventures. Be sure to look for the newly packaged and longer Harlequin Romantic Suspense stories wherever you buy books.

In the meantime, you can check out this month's adrenaline-charged reads:

CHRISTMAS CONFIDENTIAL by Marilyn Pappano and Linda Conrad

COLTON SHOWDOWN by Marie Ferrarella

O'HALLORAN'S LADY by Fiona Brand

NO ESCAPE by Meredith Fletcher

Happy reading!

Patience Bloom

Senior Editor

MARILYN PAPPANO

Holiday Protector

Chapter 1

Walking out of the prison doors for the first time was much easier than walking in.

Miri Duncan stood in the bright afternoon sun, just soaking it all in: the grass beneath her feet, the crisp December air, the gates and tall fences of the armed fortress behind her. After 432 days, she could do what she wanted—walk down the highway in either direction, sit down right where she was, do anything or nothing. She was free.

Free. Such a heady thought…and a scary one. She had to make decisions for herself now. Luckily, she'd been planning this day since the day she'd arrived at the women's correctional center. She had places to go and people to see—three, to be exact. Her sister, Sophy, in Copper Lake, Georgia, their brother, Oliver, in Asheville, North Carolina, and baby sister, Chloe, in Dothan, Alabama.

The nearest town was about a mile south along the highway, one of the guards had told her, so she turned in that direction. There she could catch a bus to Dallas, where a storage locker held some of her belongings. Then she would head to Copper Lake with a gift like Sophy had never seen.

The sound of an approaching vehicle made her step a few feet farther from the white line marking the southbound lane. She glanced over her shoulder and saw a silver pickup, a red-and-green wreath secured to its grille and large brown antlers affixed to the roof. The reminder that Christmas was only four days away surprised her. Once upon a time it had been the most exciting time of the year for her and her siblings, with a tree, decorations, parties and more gifts than they'd ever needed or even wanted. Mama had *loved* Christmas and celebrated it with a vengeance.

Until everything went wrong and neither Mama nor Miri had ever again acknowledged the day as anything but one more to get through.

Stiffening her shoulders, Miri shoved the memories back into their dark corner and focused on the days ahead. She'd had Sophy's gift ready for delivery last Christmas, before she'd found out she would be a guest of the state of Texas for the holiday. Sophy was only four years younger than Miri, so in their last months together, they'd shared the burden of caring for their family. They'd soothed the younger kids and Mama, then cried on each other's shoulders when the others slept. She was the one Miri wanted to see first. The one Miri missed most.

The sounds of another vehicle approaching caught her attention. This time she didn't bother to look but walked on, one foot scuffing the edge of the shoulder. The whine of the tires on pavement decreased, and a moment later, the hum of a powerful engine came alongside her. She didn't shift her gaze, as if ignoring the car would make its driver ignore her.

It seemed to work for a moment. The car drove past, then steered onto the shoulder, blocking her way ahead.

She stopped suddenly, hands clenching in her pockets. She knew that car. Worse, she knew its driver.

The driver's door opened slowly, and she wondered if she could run back to the prison before the man could catch her. But she would be damned if she would let him make her run. The past was done. Her debt was paid.

Lengthening her stride, she passed the car on the passenger side. Her peripheral vision caught a glimpse of black hair, a jacket that she knew smelled of old leather and felt as soft as butter. She willed him not to speak, willed herself not to hear, but that worked about as well as ignoring him.

"Hey, Miriam."

She'd switched to her middle name twelve years ago, shortening it to Miri, thinking to make a new start as a new person. He was the only person in all that time who'd called her Miriam. She did *not* like it, the way it came out *meer-e-yumm,* any more than she liked him.

"I would have been here sooner but I got held up on the way."

She kept walking.

The car door closed, then he jogged to catch up and circle around in front of her. "Aw, come on, Miriam. No grudges, right?"

She kept walking, forcing him to move backward to stay ahead.

"Hey, give me a break, huh? I was just doing my job. At least let me make it up to you now with a ride into Dallas."

She kept walking, shoving past him when he stopped, tensing at the contact, half expecting him to grab her arm or her hand. *Not* disappointed when he didn't.

"I'm just trying to be a nice guy, Miriam," he called after her.

Finally she stopped, her entire body stiff. She turned to

face him slowly, hands fisted in her pockets. "No one would mistake you for a nice guy, Montgomery."

Foolish enough to think she could be cajoled, he smiled that big-kid smile that got him pretty much anything he wanted from women of all ages, opened his arms in an expansive gesture and laid on the Texas drawl. "*You* used to think I was nice, Miriam. You thought I was *real* nice. Nice enough to kiss. Nice enough to—" His shoulders lifted in a shrug.

The kicker was, he was right. He'd been charming and sexy and funny, and he had a way of looking at a person as if she were the only thing that existed in his universe. She *had* thought he was nice. She'd thought he might be The One.

Men were put here to break our hearts, baby, her mother used to say in her rare moments of lucidity. Miri had had experience with only two—her father and Dean Montgomery—and they'd both surely done that.

"What do you want?"

His smile disappeared into a tight-lipped grimace, and he shoved his hands into his jacket pockets. Inside the left one, she knew, were his keys. Inside the other, a stash of cellophane-wrapped peppermints. Despite the chill, he was radiating heat. He always did, as if he had too much passion for his body to contain.

"Listen, Miriam, I just want to make up a little for my part in what happened. What's the harm in accepting a ride into the city from me? Hell, I'll take you wherever you want to go. It's my way of saying I'm sorry."

He sounded sincere, but Miri had too much experience with expert liars to trust him. Her father was the best liar in the world. She was a pretty good one, too. She even lied to herself and even, sometimes, believed it.

Still, she wanted to get to Georgia before doubt had a chance to win her over to its side. Doubt said she should put the gift in a box and ship it to Sophy, that Sophy didn't want to see her, probably didn't even remember her. After all, she'd been just six when Social Services had separated them. Eventually Miri had returned home with their mother, but the younger three kids had all been placed in new homes with new families.

It had been twenty years since she'd seen her siblings, twelve years since she'd had any family at all. Just once, just for a day or two, she'd like to be with someone who'd once loved her, who might think of her or even miss her from time to time.

Just once, she didn't want to be alone.

"If you say no, I'll follow you," Dean warned. "I'm stubborn that way."

She knew that for a fact. The first time he'd asked her out, she'd said no—and the second and the third. But he'd kept asking, catching her in the office, on the street outside, at the deli where she ate lunch every day, never giving up until she'd given in. Then she'd been flattered. Now she knew the real reason he'd been so persistent.

A ride to Dallas. With her guard up, what could it hurt? It would be faster than a bus, and Dean couldn't be much more annoying than a Greyhound full of strangers, could he?

"All right." She turned and marched back to the forty-some-year-old Charger that was his pride and joy, climbed into the passenger seat and fastened the seat belt, staring straight ahead. She pretended not to recognize the familiar scents of the car—age, leather, cologne, Dean. She pretended not to notice when he slid into the driver's seat and turned his all-too-familiar gaze on her. Already she regretted accepting his offer, but she reminded herself again of Sophy, of the gift and all she'd sacrificed for it.

She'd been through hell more than a few times. She could bear it once again if it meant getting to her sister sooner.

* * *

Not even 432 days in prison could make Miri any less the prettiest woman Dean had ever known. Slender, graceful, delicate features, pale blond hair, big brown eyes that held a sense of…sadness, maybe, or vulnerability. He didn't know exactly how to describe it. He just knew it had caught his interest the first time he'd ever seen her.

She didn't look like a woman who'd spent the past fourteen months in jail. She wasn't thinner than usual, paler or tougher. She wasn't any friendlier, or any less so, than he'd expected given the circumstances, but he could handle that. He had 110,000 incentives to take whatever hostility she directed his way.

Shifting into gear, he eased back on to the roadway, then kicked it up to sixty-five. With a sidelong look her way, he said, "Nice that you got out in time for Christmas. You have family expecting you somewhere?"

She gave no sign of hearing him, but he was nothing if not relentless. "I'm on my own this year. Mom and Dad are on a cruise somewhere in the Caribbean right now. Celebrating their forty-fifth anniversary."

No response.

"My sisters are all meeting at Adele's house in California, but I'm thinking three sisters, two husbands and nine kids under the age of ten are a little more holiday cheer than I want to take on." And with Miri's release coming right before the big day…

Her gaze flickered to the right as they approached a road sign—fifty-two miles to Dallas—then she went back to staring straight ahead.

It was going to be one hell of a long drive.

He let a few miles pass in silence before trying again. "Are you planning to stay in Dallas?" He didn't know where she'd lived before coming to Texas. Truth was, considering how close they'd gotten and how fast, he didn't really know a lot about her.

He'd had no clue she was the embezzler he'd been searching for.

He sure as hell hadn't known he would be instrumental in sending her to prison.

But he wouldn't change anything he'd done. She had stolen more than a million dollars from his client's insurance brokerage. She'd chosen to commit the crime and, therefore, to accept the potential punishment. If he hadn't traced the theft back to her, someone else would have.

Though maybe, if he'd known everything, he wouldn't have gone out with her.

Nah, he probably would have. He'd never been able to resist a challenge, and she'd been a major one from the start.

Getting her to say something was a new, smaller challenge. "You can try to ignore me, Miriam, but we've got about fifty miles left, and I'm not so easy to tune out."

Finally she turned her head to level a cool, unemotional gaze on him. "I spent 431 nights in a cell block with 120 other women who talked, snored or cried all night. You underestimate my ability to tune out annoying noise."

That twinge in his gut must be hunger, because he did *not* feel guilty for even one of those nights. His fingers tightening on the steering wheel, he casually said, "I never underestimated anything about you, Miriam. Except your tendency toward criminal behavior. But, hey, it paid off for you, didn't it? A million bucks isn't a bad trade for fourteen months of your time."

Her gaze sharpened, her mouth pinched, then she turned away again, this time staring out the side window.

One thing he'd never known: why she'd taken the money. She hadn't used any of it to pay for an attorney, instead pleading guilty to the charge against her. Before getting caught, she'd driven an eight-year-old Toyota and lived in a cramped apartment in a neighborhood *he* hadn't been comfortable in without his gun. She hadn't worn designer clothes, taken any vacations since she'd started working for the company or owned any electronics besides an off-brand TV. Her only jewelry had been a cheap watch, a chain with a silver heart and a plain gold wedding band.

He didn't know if it had been hers, if she'd been married or, hell, if she'd stolen it, too.

And he didn't care. All he was interested in was the ten percent finder's fee John W. Smith had offered, both to Dean and to Bud Garvin, one of Dean's competitors in the P.I. business, for the return of his money.

Dean intended to claim it.

"Remember Trish Lewis? Sat in the cubicle across from you? She got married six months ago and delivered twins two months later. Boys."

He might as well be talking to himself for all the reaction she showed. He'd expected something. Trish had been the closest to a friend Miri had had at the company. She had also, for a while, been a suspect. He might look like all charm and no substance, but he had a few skills, including the ones needed to trace all the unauthorized financial transfers back to Miri.

A short distance ahead was the entrance to the interstate, along with a half dozen fast food joints. Remembering her fondness for small, very basic burgers, he slowed and pulled into the drive-through for the golden arches. "Want something?" *Other than to be away from me?*

He thought she was going to continue the silent treatment, but as he stopped in front of the order box, she relented. "A burger."

"With cheese, right?" Though he'd never known many of the details of her life, he remembered she liked burgers with cheese, coffee with cream, onion rings instead of fries, loved hot cocoa and had a wicked sweet tooth that she indulged every evening and compensated for by skipping breakfast the next morning.

And he remembered that her kisses tasted of chocolate and rich dark roast coffee, that she smelled like jasmine and felt like the finest-woven silk.

He definitely remembered his regret that she'd been arrested before he'd been able to get far enough past her defenses to have sex. He was pretty sure it would have been the best he'd had in a long time.

Scowling, he ordered four cheeseburgers, figuring if she didn't want a second one, he could polish it off. He added pop, diet for her and high-sugar, high-caffeine for himself, then tossed in an order of fries. He could always run an extra few miles.

"What's the food like in prison? I hear both good and bad about it."

Nothing.

He let his gaze slide over her, from the top of her natural blond roots all the way down to her well-worn tennis shoes. "It doesn't seem to have hurt you."

Ah, the muscles in her jaw twitched. It wasn't much, but it *was* a response. She didn't have to be friendly. She just had to lead him to the cash.

As he pulled up to the window, she shifted to dig in her pocket, pulling out a crumpled bill. He waved it away, smiling as if she wouldn't like to claw his eyes out. "My treat."

Without protest, she put the money back.

The woman at the cash register was chunky and gray-haired and looked as if she'd had a long shift, but her smile was genuine. "Four dollars and eighteen cents is your change. Y'all have a Merry Christmas." Then she winked slyly. "Hope you find what you want under your tree Christmas morning."

Dean grinned. "I always do." He was lucky that way, and this year a hundred grand would make for the best holiday ever.

After picking up the food and drinks at the next window, he pulled into a parking space and began unwrapping one burger. He felt Miri's attention before she actually spoke.

"Can't you drive and eat?"

"When I need to, but what's the hurry?"

Her mouth pinched again, and he was pretty sure she'd barely stopped an eye roll.

"Let me remind you, Miriam, if I hadn't talked you into accepting a ride, you'd be hoofing it into town about now, then waiting for a bus. I know that because the guard told me when I went looking for you at the prison. Since you're ahead of schedule, you can spare a few minutes for a civilized meal."

This time the corners of her mouth twitched, but she maintained the flat expression. "This is your idea of a civilized meal? Even in prison we sat at tables and had utensils—nothing dangerous, of course—and napkins."

He dipped into the bag and pulled out a handful of paper. "We have napkins. And who needs utensils for hamburgers? Besides, I'm not sure I'd trust you with anything dangerous, either."

She stared at him while nibbling her burger, taking delicate little bites and chewing them thoroughly before swallowing. He'd finished his first and a handful of fries in the time it took her to eat a third of hers.

She did everything delicately. Even the smallest of movements, like brushing back a strand of hair or pursing her lips in concentration, were potently feminine and graceful, sensuous and innocent. He'd wondered a lot over the past year how much of it was an act, but he'd never been able to decide. She'd planned and carried out a complex crime, and yet she looked... Not like an angel. Heavenly beings surely didn't kiss the way she did. Like a faerie or pixie or some other make-believe creature.

"Why are you here?"

Though he saw her lips moving to form the words, it took him a moment to hear the question. With a shrug, he unwrapped the next burger. "I told you, I just wanted to say I'm sorry for the way things worked out. I know a ride's not much in exchange for sending you to prison, but—"

Her shrug was much more elegant than his. Her thin jacket, worn over a plain T-shirt, shifted and hugged her, reminding him of the curves those clothes held. Not that he'd actually seen her naked. He'd never gotten her stripped beyond her shirt, but the memory of her breasts and the small bits of lace that didn't quite cover them still hung around. He could imagine the rest. He was a man, after all.

"Like you said, you were doing your job."

That surprised him. "You don't hold it against me that I turned you in?"

She took a suck of pop before giving him that look again. That was the only real difference he'd found yet: that flat lack of expression. Just how bad had prison been to wipe all the emotion from her face?

"Am I a success or failure among your cases?"

"I caught you. What do you think?"

"But you didn't recover the money."

"I wasn't hired to get the money back." *Not that time, at least.* "My orders were to find who was funneling Mr. Smith's money into overseas accounts and stop it. I did."

"Mr. Smith." Her tone was almost disinterested, but faintly, barely noticeable, scorn underlay the words.

When she didn't continue, Dean finished his second

burger, then asked, "So if you don't hold the whole arrest and prison thing against me, then we're good, right? Friends again?"

Making and keeping friends had never been an easy thing for Miri. When Social Services yanked her from home to home for nearly a year, then she and Mom had had to stay on the move the next seven years to avoid their notice, she hadn't had friends—just people who came and went from her life. By the time she was old enough that no one cared whether she had a stable home or slept under a bridge, she'd lost the ability to make friends. Everyone she'd loved had abandoned her. Everyone, even her mother, had gone on to a better life without her. How could she have trusted anyone to stay?

All her adult relationships had been superficial—the occasional boyfriend for occasional sex, office chatter with the people whose desks surrounded hers, exchanging guarded hellos with her neighbor. Finding Sophy, Oliver and Chloe would give her back that ability to connect, she'd thought, and so she'd searched and plotted, but she'd wondered. Was it already too late? Was she too damaged to have normal relationships again?

With Dean, she'd begun to believe the answer was no. She'd trusted him. She'd connected with him. She'd believed he wanted her, cared for her. Then she'd opened the door to him the evening of their last date, and there he'd stood with two detectives behind him. He had listened to them read her rights, had watched them lead her away in handcuffs, and he hadn't said a word.

As they'd both said, he'd just been doing the job Smith had hired him for. She'd been well aware when she came up with her scheme that her freedom was at risk. But she hadn't known her heart was at risk, too. She hadn't counted on

Dean Montgomery romancing her, gaining her trust, making her think he might love her, all for the sake of his job.

That was what she held against him. What she couldn't forgive.

Friends again? "That's not going to happen. But I do appreciate the ride." She took the last bite of her cheeseburger, savoring the taste as she carefully wadded the wrapper into a neat ball with the napkin and straw paper inside. Deliberately she turned her head to the side again, glancing from restaurant to gas station to passing traffic. So many people with places to go, families to see, friends to celebrate with. She felt so alone, but that was nothing new. If men were put on earth to break women's hearts, maybe *she'd* been put here just to have her heart broken. Maybe she was one of those sad people destined to live their lives in quiet despair, so needy of companionship that they'd take it from anyone or so fearful that they couldn't risk it with anyone.

Now, wasn't that a cheery happy-holidays thought?

"I am sorry, Miriam."

"Okay." She locked her gaze on a minivan with out-of-state plates at the gas station next door, kids piling out of the back, herded inside by their father while their mother pumped gas. Suitcases were lashed to the baggage carrier on the roof, and piles of brightly wrapped gifts were visible in the rear storage space. Did those kids realize how lucky they were? Did they know they would look back in twenty years and forget the long hours of traveling and the squabbling and just remember that they'd been together?

Probably not. Look at Dean. He had his entire family, minus parents, ready to welcome him into their midst for Christmas, and instead he chose to stay here in Texas and... what? What use could he possibly have for Miri now?

The money, of course. It was only reasonable to assume that as soon as she got out of prison, she'd take the money and run. Returning it to John W. Smith—*Mister* Smith, she scoffed—would turn her case from merely solved to successfully tied up, restitution made and everyone happy except Miri.

In Dean's dreams. That money belonged to her and nothing—no one, she added as he started the engine to back out—was going to take it away.

Once they'd merged into traffic on the interstate, he turned on the radio and for a moment, Christmas music blasted into the car. One good thing about prison: she hadn't been forced to endure six weeks of "Jingle Bell Rock," "I'll Be Home for Christmas," or "The Christmas Song." Before she finished the thought, though, he switched to a CD, Eric Clapton singing the blues. Much more appropriate to her mood.

They'd gone through that and a Joe Bonamassa disc before Dean spoke again. He was no longer making an effort at charming her. "Where do you want to go?"

She looked around and saw that they'd covered the distance into the city while the music distracted her. "My old neighborhood."

His look was sharp, but he said nothing. He hadn't liked the area around her apartment, or so he'd said. She needed to find someplace safer, less scary. As if he'd cared.

She wouldn't forgive him for making her think that. Wouldn't forgive herself for being so gullible.

The traffic, the crowdedness, the buildings looming everywhere disconcerted her, knotting her stomach. She'd lived her entire life in cities. They were wonderful places for getting lost, for being anonymous, but suddenly she was having trouble filling her lungs. Once she'd made contact with her sisters and brother, she would find a small town to settle in, maybe near them if they were open to that, maybe somewhere out west where she could finally start that brand-new life she'd been longing for since she was ten years old.

"Now where?"

She looked around again and recognized the down-on-its-luck neighborhood she'd called home for two years. On the four corners where they waited at a red light sat the market where she'd bought huge cups of diet pop more for the finely crushed ice than the drink, the dry cleaner where she'd dropped off her work clothes every Friday, the gas station where she'd filled her car when she forgot to do so at the cheaper stations on the way to work and a bar that did steady business all day and into the night.

Three blocks away was one of the storage facilities she'd rented more than a year ago.

"You can let me out here."

"Come on." He shot her an impatient look. "You don't expect me to just leave you on a street corner."

"I don't expect anything of you." She'd learned that the hard way.

"I told you I'd take you wherever you want to go."

"I want out here."

"Miriam—" A horn blasted behind them, and he scowled into the rearview mirror before turning the corner and pulling to the curb. "You don't even have a place to stay."

"I had access to both mail and telephones in prison. I took care of that." She unbuckled the seat belt and reached for the door handle. His hand on her arm stopped her.

"Tell me where you're staying and I'll take you there."

The smile that curved her lips as she turned to look at him was cool and a reminder of the chill deep inside her. "Why would I want you to know where I'm staying? Given our past—"

"You said you didn't hold the job against me."

"I don't."

"Then I don't get—" He removed his hand to drag his fingers through his hair. "I said I'm sorry, damn it."

She stared at him a long time, committing every detail to memory—as if she'd ever forgotten. "Some things can't be fixed with an apology." Her father had taught her that. *I'm sorry, but I can't live this way any longer.* And later, *I'm sorry, but I can't take you with me.* Later still, *I'm sorry, but she's not my problem. Neither are you. I have a life, you know. Obligations.*

She, Sophy, Oliver and Chloe hadn't even ranked as obligations to their father.

Mister Smith.

Before Dean could say anything else—or, worse, touch her again—she opened the door, climbed out, then closed it again with a solid *thunk*. She was in Dallas. Sophy's gift was only three blocks away. Dean Montgomery was about to drive out of her life forever.

She was ready to take the next step, and she did it literally, turning to cross the sidewalk and go inside the market. The clerk behind the counter was the same elderly Vietnamese woman who'd worked there a year ago. She looked up from the customer she was waiting on, and a rote smile flashed across her face. Not a sign that she remembered Miri, but just the way she greeted every customer.

Miri browsed up and down the aisles, keeping an eye on the street outside. Dean sat there for a long time, long enough to change the clerk's expression from polite to suspicious. Miri picked up a couple of candy bars, a bag of potato chips and filled a monster cup with ice and diet pop, and finally Dean drove away from the curb. Satisfaction settled over her. Weird how it had a kind of disappointed feel to it.

She was the lone customer at the counter when she paid, adding a last-minute purchase of a ball cap. Sliding her change into her pocket, she ripped the tag from the hat, then picked up the bag and the pop before asking, "Would it be okay if I go out the back door? There's a man…" She gestured toward the street, even though the Charger was gone.

The woman's gaze narrowed, but after a moment she nodded toward the rear door that led into the storeroom, then to the back door. As Miri was walking that way, the woman murmured, "Welcome back."

Miri stumbled, a sharp sting in her chest making her breath catch. The woman remembered her, even though her entire adult life she'd worked so hard at being forgettable that she'd actually become it. "Th-thank you."

The storeroom's heavy steel door opened into an alley that stank of refuse. Clamping the hat on her head, hair gathered up beneath it, she removed her jacket and shoved it into the plastic bag. As camouflage went, it wasn't much, but it was better than nothing. She walked to the far end of the street, eyes shifting constantly, then turned left for a block. There was no sign of Dean anywhere, thank God.

There were no decorations attached to the light poles, but about half the businesses she passed had some sign of the holiday: wreaths on doors, paintings of Santa, reindeer and plump snowmen on the plate-glass windows. Snippets of the Muppets singing carols came from one open door as she passed, too sudden to tune out.

At the next alley, she turned again, zigging and zagging until she reached the storage facility. The chain-link fence was lined with Christmas lights, even its sagging sections, and life-size replicas formed a manger scene in the yellow grass outside the office door. Overhead, garish red-and-green lights on a sign flashed out greetings and Bible quotes.

She'd rented the smallest-size locker eighteen months ago, paying cash for two years, to store what few belongings she'd brought to Dallas with her: clothes, keepsakes, books. On good days, her mother had read the books to them every night. On bad days, her flair for the dramatic soared over the top, funny and entertaining until they—at least Miri and Sophy—had realized the behavior was a sign that something ugly was about to happen. Those were the days their father had turned cold, eventually sending their mother to bed where she cried inconsolably. A day, or two or three, later, she would emerge from the bedroom, smiling, happy once again, but each time more fragile, like a delicate glass ball that might shatter.

Miri opened the door and walked into the space, barely bigger than a closet. By the light of the dim bulb overhead, she pried the lid from a plastic tub, took the backpack off the top and began stuffing it with clothes. She located the few bits of her mother's jewelry she'd been able to hang on to and zipped them into the pack, then added Sophy's favorite of the thin, flat storybooks. She traded her jacket for a sturdy coat from another tub before opening the bin labeled Dishes and taking out the final, most important item.

Boo was close to thirty years old, the size of a small child, and he showed the wear of a well-loved bear. His button eyes didn't match, and his fur was rubbed bare in places. One ear stood straight, the other flopping over, and thick black *X*'s stitched on his left arm showed Miri's brief foray into a surgical career.

To most people, he would look old, worn and worthless.

But most people didn't know about the quarter of a million dollars stuffed into his middle.

Slinging the backpack over one shoulder, she wrapped both arms around Boo's neck, locked up and headed back the way she'd come. It wasn't more than a mile's walk to the bus station, where she hoped she could catch a bus heading east.

She was afraid to even hope much for a good reception when she got there.

But at least Sophy would surely welcome Boo.

Chapter 2

When a song about decking the halls came on the radio, Dean jabbed the button to shut it off. He'd like to deck something, but it sure wasn't a freaking hall. What kind of P.I. was he if he couldn't even follow one woman who stood out in every crowd she'd ever been in?

Two, no more than three minutes—that was how long he'd been gone from the convenience store, just long enough to drive down the block and make a U-turn, and when he'd come back, Miri was already gone. Guessing she'd gone out the back door, he'd driven for an hour up and down the streets, through alleys and three times past the apartments where she used to live. He'd seen few blondes and none that was even vaguely familiar.

For the past hour he'd driven in widening circles, so focused on the women on the street that he felt like a perv. Where would she go? She had no friends in Dallas, no family. With her lack of ties, logic dictated that after leaving prison, she would get the hell out of Texas and go someplace where she could enjoy Mr. Smith's money in peace.

But where? He'd gone over every conversation they'd ever had, trying to remember if she'd mentioned any place she would like to visit, any place she missed, but he came up blank. He'd talked about the future—in general terms, since he was posing as the new IT guy at John W. Smith Global and restricted from telling too much truth—but she'd never said a word about her plans. No *I'd love to be soaking up rays on a Caribbean beach* or *hiking in the Rockies* or *eating my mom's pierogies in Michigan.*

So, continuing with logic... To leave Dallas, she needed transportation. This close to Christmas, airline tickets were tough to come by. Buses and trains, he had no idea. She no longer owned the old Toyota, and—

She'd asked the prison guard where she could catch a bus. When he'd wondered where she was going, she'd shrugged and said, *Dallas, for a start.* He'd directed her to the town nearest the prison, where she would have caught a Greyhound, if Dean hadn't shown up, which would have delivered her directly to the bus station in Dallas—*for a start.*

Since he didn't have any other clues, he headed toward the station. Traffic was heavy, and tension made him grip the steering wheel hard when he was moving and drum his fingers on it when he wasn't. He didn't want to lose his shot at the finder's fee. More than that, he didn't want to disappoint Mr. Smith. If not for the business he'd thrown Dean's way, the P.I. office would still be a barely-breaking-even one-man job. Now he had three employees, and he finished each month with a nice bit of change in the bank. He owed Mr. Smith.

He didn't like leaving a case unfinished.

And he especially didn't like being outsmarted.

The bus station was busier than he expected. He couldn't

imagine a much worse fate than being stuck on a bus for endless hours, with no control over who sat beside him or what they did while they sat there. Plus, it put him in mind of grade school when he'd had to ride the bus every day, the target of three kids who'd lived to torment him. One, no surprise, had ended up in prison. The second was a career non-commissioned officer in the Marine Corps, and the third had become a minister. Holy crap.

Finding a parking space half a block away, Dean locked the car and tugged his jacket tighter as he walked to the station. According to the weather guys, a cold spell was moving into Texas today on its way east. There was talk about snow for Christmas, something he could definitely live without.

He walked through the terminal, scanning passengers. There were couples, families, people traveling alone, some toting bags of gifts, others with nothing more than a backpack or duffel, one clutching a big stuffed bear. None of them was Miri. After waiting in line, he showed the woman at the ticket counter Miri's picture. Dorrie, with big hair and no smile, flashed it around at her coworkers, then handed it back without a word.

Okay, the bus hunch was wrong. No one could have sold a ticket to Miri in the past few hours—the past few *months*—and not remembered her.

He'd been so smug when he'd caught sight of her outside the prison. The day had sure gone downhill fast since then.

"Hey, doll." The female voice came from behind him and was unfamiliar, so he didn't even look around until someone touched his arm.

He turned his head, saw air, then lowered his gaze a foot or more to see a plump face smiling at him. The woman was as big around as she was tall, with brown curls, a Rudolph pin on her Christmas-themed sweater and earrings shaped like Christmas trees that flashed tiny multicolored lights. There was even a snowman bow in her hair.

"Can I see that picture? I just got a glimpse of it at the counter."

"Sure." He pulled the photo from his pocket, grateful he'd gotten the snapshot of Miri before her arrest and didn't have to use her booking photo. "Have you seen her?"

Instead of answering right away, she studied the photo, then him. "Pretty girl. Who is she?"

"My girlfriend. We got into an argument, and she decided to take the bus to her folks' house instead of riding with me." He was good at lying, a skill he'd cultivated for his work. It had never bothered him before, but now guilt twinged inside him. Must be the holidays.

"When my husband and I—" she gestured to a gray-haired man wearing a similar sweater and, no kidding, reindeer antlers on his head "—got here, I had to go to the little girls' room, and I'm pretty sure this is the blonde who was in there. You should never argue during the holidays, doll. Have you bought her something nice to make up for it?"

"There's lots better ways to make up for it than presents." Her husband grinned at Dean, and his wife rewarded him with an elbow to the stomach.

"Did you see where she went when she left the bathroom?" Dean asked.

The woman stood on tiptoe to scan the room. "She was wearing a blue coat and a tan baseball cap. Had all that pretty hair hidden away. Oh, and she was carrying a huge teddy bear. You'd think I would have remembered that first, wouldn't you?"

Teddy bear. Dean had seen a teddy bear, arms wrapped around it as if it were precious. He spun to look in that direction, but it had moved, so he scanned the room again.

No buses had pulled out since he'd walked in, so she had to still be there, but where?

"There." The woman tugged his arm, then pointed out the front window at a slender figure in a blue jacket, the ragged head of a bear peeking up over one shoulder. "She must have needed some air. Go make up with her—and y'all have a really good Christmas."

"Thanks. You, too." Dodging passengers, Dean reached the door in seconds, stepping out in time to get blasted by a cold wind. He didn't call Miri's name—he wouldn't be surprised if she tried to ditch him again—but headed toward the massive concrete pillar where she stood.

He hadn't taken more than a few steps when a man came into view from the cover of the pillar and took hold of Miri's left arm. She shook her head and stepped backward, trying to pull away without any luck. Instead, the man tightened his grip and started to drag her away from the station.

Just a random mugging? Or did the guy work for Bud Garvin? Dean didn't recognize him, but then, Garvin used a lot of muscle. It was tough to keep track of them all.

Dean quickened his pace until he was jogging, his right hand automatically going to the pistol tucked in his waistband in back. "Hey," he called. "What are you doing?"

Miri's expression when she turned was relief tinged with fright. It did something to his gut—her being scared, grabbed by a stranger. It made him queasy, but worse—for the other guy—it pissed him off. Retrieving the stolen money from her was one thing, but roughing her up? Frightening her? That wasn't part of the deal.

He stopped beside her, taking hold of her other arm, fixing his gaze on the man. "I'd suggest you remove your hand before I remove it for you."

The guy grinned, and from the right a fist smashed into Dean's jaw with enough force to sprawl him on the ground.

He didn't have time to let go of Miri, and she tumbled with him as a second man stepped out of the shadows of the pillar. He gave his hand a shake, then flexed his fingers. "Damn. Lucky for you, I didn't break anything."

"I tried to warn you!" Miri snapped.

Warn? She hadn't said a word, had just looked like a modern damsel in distress, body trembling, eyes shifting, head shaking the tiniest bit.… "That's what you call a warning? Next time try screaming, 'Dean, he's not alone.'"

The first man smirked. "Dean, I'm not alone. Now, this pretty little girl is our Christmas present to ourselves. We found her first, so we get to unwrap her. You, get up and get out of here. Blondie's coming with us."

Slowly Dean sat up. His jaw was throbbing, and his left elbow hurt from contact with the pavement, which was damn cold for sitting on. Sliding his right hand behind him, he rubbed his jaw with his left hand, worked it from side to side and decided it wasn't broken, though he might have trouble eating the big thick steak he'd planned on for Christmas dinner.

"Listen, guys," he said pleasantly, despite the pain. His jaw might move side to side just fine, but up and down hurt. "There are a lot of people in the terminal, and some of them are probably watching through the windows. On top of that, there are cameras everywhere. And on top of *that,* I have my right hand on an HK .45 compact that is guaranteed to make your Christmas very unmerry." He paused to ease to his feet and pull Miri up, too, then suggested, "You don't want the kind of trouble Blondie will bring. Turn around, walk away and find someone else."

The first man moved as if he were going to argue, but the second one waved him back. After a long, silent moment, he gestured again, spun on his heel and walked away.

Miri clung to Dean's hand as the first man followed.

Thirty feet away, he looked back, giving an obscene wave, then they turned the corner and disappeared from sight.

"Do you really have a gun?" she whispered.

"I really do." He grinned at her. "A really big one. And I'm really accurate with it, too."

When a moment passed without either man coming back, she abruptly let go of him and stepped back, burying both hands in the bear's ragged fur. "Thank you."

"Aw, I bet it kills you to say that to me. My car's back that way—"

She took another step back. "I'm not going with you."

"You think I'm gonna let you go back inside and give those guys another chance? No way, Miriam. Wherever you're going, I'll take you."

"Let me?" she echoed, holding the bear tighter. "I'm a free woman. I can do pretty much anything I want. The State of Texas says so."

"Yeah, well, my state of mind says you can't. Jeez, you don't know how those guys were planning to celebrate. They could have raped you, beat you or *killed* you. You think I want that on my conscience because I couldn't persuade you to be reasonable?"

Regretting the last word instantly, he reached out before she could find the words to slice him to ribbons. "Strike that. Bad choice of words. I don't think you're being unreasonable at all. I just—" He dragged his fingers through his hair, then exhaled loudly. A thin vapor formed in the air between them. "I owe you, Miriam. Let me take you and that god-awful bear wherever you're going. You don't even have to tell me exactly where. You want to go to California? I'll take you to L.A. You want to go to Colorado, we'll go to Denver. You can make the rest of the trip on your own then if that's what you want. Just let me do that much for you, okay? It'll be my Christmas gift to you."

She stared at him a long moment, her eyes narrowed, still annoyed by that "reasonable" comment, then she started walking toward the Charger down the street. Before he caught up with her, he heard her mutter.

"Boo's not god-awful. He's beautiful. And you question *my* reason?"

Miri tossed her pack into the backseat, fastened the seat belt, then gathered Boo close again. She was grateful to be out of the cold, to be back in one of the few familiar places in her life. With the tinted windows obscuring her from anyone outside and Dean settling into the driver's seat, she felt safe.

It was stupid to think of Dean and safety in the same sentence. He would never physically hurt her, she knew that, but he'd deceived and disappointed her before, and those kind of wounds were usually far more difficult to recover from.

Okay, so she just wouldn't let herself be vulnerable. She'd spent two-thirds of her life on guard, protecting and hiding herself from emotional attachments. She'd learned too well the cost of caring and the inevitability of losing. The only person she could truly count on was herself.

But that didn't mean she couldn't accept help from someone when it best suited her. She was cautious, not stupid.

He started the engine and turned the heat to high. Cool air from the vents warmed quickly, chasing the chill from her feet.

When he made no move to put the car into gear, she glanced his way and found him watching her. "What?" she asked automatically.

"Where are we going?"

His use of *we* made her stomach tighten. They weren't a *we* and never really had been. She hadn't been part of a *we* for so long that she didn't know if she could even remember how. "East."

"Can you be a little more specific? The east side of Dallas? East Texas? East of the Mississippi?"

It took a swallow or two for her to force the answer out. "Georgia. Atlanta." Copper Lake was only ninety minutes or so from there. Surely she could travel that far alone without getting accosted, or maybe she'd even call Sophy to meet her there. Her sister might not want her showing up in her hometown, anyway, especially on the eve of the biggest family holiday of the year.

He pulled out onto the street. "Do you mind if we stop by my place first to get some clothes?"

She didn't want to stop anywhere, not even to eat or spend the night, but he was doing her this favor, so the least she could do was be agreeable. "No problem." Then she stared out the side window.

Was this really a favor? Did he really care about anything that had happened between them? Or was the money his ulterior motive?

People didn't do her favors. You had to have some kind of relationship before favors came into the picture, and she didn't have those. So he was probably looking for the money.

That was okay, she told herself, but the tightening in her chest seemed to disagree.

She'd been to his apartment a time or two when they were dating—when he was working her as a suspect. It was only about ten miles from hers, but another galaxy in terms of hope. The houses were older and well maintained, the businesses more prosperous, the streets safer. Bad things could happen anywhere—she knew that from her own experiences growing up in an upper-class Asheville neighborhood—but bad seemed less likely to happen here than in her own area.

He rented a second-story apartment in one of those old, well-maintained houses, with a side set of stairs and a grandmotherly landlady occupying the first floor. GranMare, she'd called herself, the nickname the first of her fifteen grandchildren had given her when he shortened Grandma Mary, and the evening they'd met, she'd greeted Miri with a huge smile and an invitation to the next family dinner.

"You need to come in," Dean said as he shut off the engine.

"I was planning to." It was cold outside, and nearly getting kidnapped had shaken her confidence. It was flimsy enough, given her mission, that another hard shake would shatter it, and she'd take Boo and his bucks and beat it to the nearest hiding place she could find.

Lightposts illuminated the street, but even without them, the Christmas decorations would have shown their way to the base of the sturdy stairs. Even the handrail was wrapped with clear white bulbs casting pale shadows on the creamy peach siding.

Miri started up the steps behind Dean, remembering the bite of the wind as she, Sophy and their mother had wrapped multicolored lights around the porch railings of their house. Brightly colored twinklers that could make you dizzy with delight had been Mom's favorite, and a big fresh-cut pine, and small paper bags half filled with sand that anchored a flickering candle lining the steps.

To shut out the memory, she forced her focus to the present. "How is GranMare?"

"Hasn't changed a bit. If she catches sight of you, just be prepared, we're not getting away without a mug of her mulled cider and a plate of Christmas candy."

The idea sounded too appealing for a woman who was guarding herself from emotional entanglements. Miri stared grimly at each step, placing her feet lightly, trying to be no more than a shadow in the night.

By the time she reached the top, Dean had unlocked the door and gone on in. She stepped inside, closed the door behind her and waited. For a guy who lived alone, he had pretty good taste. The sofa was plain brown leather, taking no attention from the beautiful Persian rug on the floor, its weaving as bare in places as Boo's fur. The smaller pieces—dining table, chairs, curio tables, bookcases—had been passed down from various relatives, and he remembered which came from whom.

His furniture had a better pedigree than she did.

She'd noted the holiday decorations and the fragrance of cinnamon drifting from a nearby unlit candle, and her gaze was skimming over photographs on the fireplace mantel when it stopped suddenly on a simple wood frame holding a picture of her. Slowly she tiptoed across the room to the rug, but she didn't go any closer.

It *was* her, taken sixteen months earlier when they'd gone to some sort of street fair. She wore a sleeveless dress in a watercolor pattern, and the high-heeled sandals that hadn't seemed such a good idea after two hours of walking dangled from her fingers. And she was smiling, really brightly happily smiling. She didn't remember the exact moment, but she did know what she'd been thinking.

This might be the guy. The one who won't break my heart.

So much for hope or, in her case, more likely wishful thinking.

Dean's steps sounded on the wood planks of the hall floor, giving her a second to hurry back to the door. One arm wrapped around Boo's neck, she shoved her free hand into her pocket and tried to look as if she wasn't wondering why he'd not only kept the photo but displayed it among pictures of friends and family. Was it his gold medal for solving the embezzling case?

"You sure you don't want to spend the night here, then start out in the morning?" Dean asked even as he began shutting off lights.

She glanced at the clock. It wasn't even seven-thirty yet. They could cover about two hundred miles by eleven…or she could sit here in the living room, pretending the photo wasn't there, biting her tongue to keep from asking him why it was there. "The roads are lit, and that piece-of-junk car of yours has this neat thing called headlights that allow you to drive as well in the dark as in daytime."

"Piece of junk?" he echoed. "That car is a classic. Do you know how many hours I spent restoring it? How much money I put into it? How many offers I've gotten from guys wanting to buy it?"

"Yeah, yeah." She opened the door as he checked the living room and kitchen, then came up behind her. "You say classic, I say piece of junk."

"It takes nerve for a woman who's holding on to a butt-ugly teddy bear like it's gold to criticize my car."

Again, she was quiet on the stairs, making the thuds of his boots behind her sound like mini-explosions. They made it to the sidewalk and then to the car without notice. Maybe GranMare's hearing wasn't what it used to be.

As they drove out of the homey family neighborhood, Miri realized she would never see that house or its neighbors again. Once they reached Atlanta, she would never see Dean again.

Maybe, her inner voice whispered snidely. *You thought you'd never see him again when you went to prison, and there he was today. You thought you'd never see him again after he let you off at the market, and there he was at the bus station. Do you really believe he's going to drive you all the way to Atlanta and leave and not look back?*

That might not be his plan, but it was hers. She intended to make sure it happened just that way. No matter how much Dean wanted the money, it was hers, and Sophy's,

Oliver's and Chloe's. There was no way anyone was keeping it from them.

Though John W. Smith had managed quite well for more than twenty years.

Guess we were an obligation after all, weren't we, Daddy?

Chapter 3

"I don't suppose you know how to get to Atlanta."

Miri glanced at Dean, the man who often worked for her father, who spoke of him with respect. Did he have any idea how Mr. Smith had abandoned his first family?

"You go east." When he snorted, she shrugged. "I didn't need to know. I intended to let the bus driver figure it out. So, driver, figure it out."

"Feel under your seat. There should be an atlas there. I'll drive, you navigate." The dash lights made his smirk easy to see. "We'll be a team."

This time she snorted. The only team she'd ever been part of was Team Mom, first with her siblings and then eight years by herself.

"I saw a T-shirt somewhere I'm gonna get you. Says 'Doesn't play well with others.'"

"Especially with people who lie," she muttered.

"Hey, I wasn't the only one keeping secrets when we

were together. I was working undercover. You were stealing money from your boss. I think that makes my lies a little more righteous."

Righteous. John W. Smith had transformed himself into a very righteous man—respectable business owner, church deacon, city leader, adoring husband and loving father. *Father,* to two daughters and two sons, children whom he showered with every privilege money could buy. Apparently, his first family had just been practice. By all appearances, he'd gotten it right the second time.

Miri didn't believe there was a single thing righteous about Smith besides his arrogance. She knew better.

"No defense for that?" Dean asked when time had passed without a response. He shifted his gaze from the street to Miri, staring blankly into the distance. She'd always kept things from him. He'd known that practically from the start. He'd thought it might have been about her family, since she'd never admitted having one. Or maybe some boyfriend or husband had run around on her and broken her heart. Maybe she'd suffered traumas that he couldn't imagine.

But she'd always been quiet, cautious, keeping him at arm's length. She'd been wary, skittish, but he'd known with time and patience, he could break through those walls she'd put up around herself.

Once he'd figured out that she was the embezzler he was looking for, time had suddenly run out.

"I pleaded guilty when I was arrested, and I served my sentence. I don't need to defend anything I've done to you."

Dean's fingers flexed tighter on the wheel as he turned on to a freeway ramp. Why hadn't she fought the charges? God knows she'd had money to hire an attorney. She could have gotten a shorter sentence, maybe even skated on the charge completely. Who knew what a jury would do when presented with a mega-rich man like Mr. Smith versus a delicate, beautiful young woman who could pass for an angel atop a Christmas tree?

But there was one more important question, and he asked it without thinking. "Why did you do it?"

"I *was* guilty."

"Not the plea. Why did you embezzle the money?" In his business, the *why* didn't usually matter. His clients asked for proof, and he gave it to them. The rest—retaliatory action, prosecution, restitution—was up to the clients or the justice system. But this time, the *why* had nagged at him. It had never gone away.

"That's no one's business but mine."

In the dim light, he thought she mouthed a few additional words, but if he asked her to repeat them, she'd probably give him the cold shoulder again.

"So one day, Miriam Duncan, who'd never had so much as a parking ticket, went to work and decided to steal $1.1 million dollars from the boss. How does that happen? How do you make the decision to go from a lifetime of law abiding to embezzling a boatload of money? Is it the same way you decide to wear red instead of blue? Sneakers instead of boots? To buy a Toyota instead of a Chevy?" He watched her from the corner of his eye for a hint of a reaction but got none. "I'll tell you, Miriam, I've been dealing with less-than-scrupulous people my whole adult life, and I've gotta believe there's more to it than that. Something important must have pushed you to that decision. Something desperate, something traumatic."

Her response was slow in coming and phony as hell. Her voice was light, almost lighthearted, but she was holding the bear so tightly it would squeal if it had a real mouth. "Sorry. No desperation, no trauma. Just plain greed."

Dean couldn't remember ever seeing the bear at her apartment, but then, he hadn't ever been inside her bedroom—not for lack of desire—and wasn't that the likely place for a security blanket/bear? What thirty-year-old wanted her aged, worn snuggly on display for visitors and dates to see?

His was neatly tucked away in a box at the back of the closet shelf. It was a rabbit, once white with pink satin ears and a fluffy tail. Now it was an odd shade of age and dirty little boy, the pink had faded to a noncolor and only a few threads remained of the tail. His name was Bunny, and Dean had no doubt Miri wouldn't believe he existed without seeing him for herself.

With an effort, he forced his attention back to the conversation. "If it was greed, why didn't you spend the money? Why didn't you buy a better car, find a decent place to live, dress better, take vacations, live in luxury?"

Slowly she turned to meet his gaze. "Maybe I didn't have the chance. Maybe that's what I plan to do now."

Not if he could help it.

"So you're going to leave me in Atlanta and… What? Catch a flight to some obscure tropical island where you can lie on the beach and have a handsome cabana boy bringing you iced tea and dessert all day? Because if you'll take me with you, I'll be happy to play cabana boy for a while." He was joking, of course. Sort of. Though the idea of endless days on a warm beach watching Miri relax in the sun in a skimpy bikini… And, just to be safe, he *had* grabbed his passport when he was packing. He wasn't about to be left standing in Hartsfield-Jackson Atlanta International watching her fly away for good.

"You can play all sorts of roles, can't you? How good are you with the strong, silent type?"

He grinned. "I do strong great, but I'm never silent. Too little time, too many interesting things to say."

"I promise you, I have no plans to be interesting."

"That's okay. You're interesting even when you're quiet."

She gave him another look, one he was pretty sure meant she didn't believe a word he said, but he let it slide.

It took a couple of freeway shifts, but soon they were on I-20 headed east. Wind buffeted the car, and when he touched the window, the glass was frigid. The front had officially arrived, he'd guess. Hopefully, the snow would stay a few hours behind them.

Not that he would mind being snowed in somewhere with Miri.

"They're saying Dallas might have snow for Christmas. We were spending the holidays in Colorado with my grandparents before I ever saw a really white Christmas." When she gave no response, he said, "Personally, I thought it was overrated. Cold, wet, stuck in the house with a convention of Montgomerys. I was never so glad to see dead grass and gray concrete again in my life."

Her death grip on the bear had eased, and now she was gently, absently stroking it. Who would have ever guessed he'd be jealous of an ugly bear?

"Did you have white Christmases where you grew up?"

He didn't expect her to answer, but after a hesitation, she did. "Often enough that it wasn't special." Another pause, then another surprise. "My mother loved snow for the holidays. She said it made everything so much more Christmassy."

Loved. Said. Past tense because it was, simply, the past? Or because Mom was no longer around to love anything?

"What else made it Christmassy? Lights, wreaths, big red bows?"

"Candles, holly, mistletoe, evergreen garlands and carols all the time." Her next words slipped out quietly, as if she were talking to herself. "She did a truly horrid rendition of "Rudolph the Red-Nosed Reindeer." And she made us watch the Burl Ives cartoon every year even though it freaked out all of us kids."

Ah, a nugget of data: in addition to a mother, she'd also had at least two siblings. More personal information than he'd ever gotten from her before. "Are you the oldest?"

"Yeah, I am—" Abruptly her gaze cut to him. "What does it matter?"

He lifted his shoulders in a shrug. "I'm just making conversation. You know all about my family." They were a big part of his life and so a big part of his conversations. "We've got a lot of hours ahead of us in the car. We've got to talk about something."

No, we don't. He heard the words in the turning away of her head as clearly as if she'd said them. Did she ever talk about her family to anyone, or was it just him she didn't trust with knowledge of them? The possibility sent a shaft of regret through him.

The silence was heavy as they drove on. At some point, she positioned the bear against the window and rested her head on it. After a while, Dean figured she'd fallen asleep, and he was about to do the same. It was getting hard to hear his yawns over the growling of his stomach. When a sign for the next exit showed a choice of motels and fast-food places, he slowed and took it.

Miri roused in the seat beside him, looking around. "Do we need gas?"

"We need food and sleep." Of course she opened her mouth to protest, but he cut her off. "I'm tired. I'm hungry. So are you. We're not driving all night. I offered you a ride. I didn't put the safety of my car on the line to get you there a few hours faster." To say nothing of their own safety. Wherever she was going, she had to be alive to get there.

"Trade places. You can sleep while I drive."

He stopped at the end of the exit ramp sign before giving her an incredulous look. "You're kidding, right? *No one* drives my car but my mechanic and me."

"Oh, come on, it's just a car." She scrubbed her fingers through her hair. "I've been driving since I was twenty. Ignition, gas, brake, turn signals—it's all the same, even on old junkers like this."

He turned into a parking lot that contained a waffle place at one end, a motel at the other and a gas station in between. The Vacancy sign, minus a few letters, alternated with messages for peace on earth, breakfast twenty-four hours a day and cheap gas. "Let's make a deal. You quit criticizing my car, and I won't mention again how ugly that bear is. Okay?"

Her gaze narrowed, her mouth thinned, she nodded.

As he stopped in front of the motel, he shut off the engine, then pocketed the keys. Registering wouldn't take more than a few minutes, but that was long enough for her to leave him standing in the cold wind alone.

"Get two rooms," she instructed when he opened the door.

"Yeah." More appropriately, he murmured after slamming the door, "Yeah, right."

Of course he got only one room. That didn't surprise Miri at all. The fact that it had two beds in it should have surprised her—didn't most men take advantage of women whenever given the chance?—but it really didn't. Dean was persistent, no doubt about that, but he'd always been gentlemanly about it. He had never behaved badly.

Unless she counted the lies and the pretense.

And then she'd have to count her own thefts and pretense. She never should have gotten involved with him, no matter how charmingly persistent he'd been. She'd *known* there was no room for a man in her life. But his attention had been so flattering, and she'd been needy.

The room was clean, though it smelled musty, rather like her pajamas. The shorts and T-shirt had been packed away for eighteen months after being laundered. But that was okay. She didn't mind, and Dean didn't care.

As soon as he'd taken her to the room, he'd left again to get food. She'd told him she wasn't hungry, but her stomach had rumbled loud enough to make a liar of her. She hoped he was the kind who could eat and fall into bed. She didn't want to waste any time unwinding. The sooner they slept, the sooner they could get on the road again.

She sat on the bed farthest from the door, Boo tucked beside her. The sound of Elvis singing "Blue Christmas" filtered faintly from somewhere. Never one of her favorite songs, especially not right now. She switched on the television to drown out the tune, channeling through holiday movies to commercials blaring gift-giving ideas to twenty-four-hour news. She muted it and turned to the program guide to find something definitively non-holiday.

When three sharp raps sounded at the door, she stiffened, then gave herself a mental shake and went to undo the chain lock. Dean came in, shivering and carrying a couple of bags of pure sensory heaven. Hamburgers, French fries, onion rings and, nearly overpowered by the other aromas, hot cocoa.

She loved hot cocoa.

"Damn, it's cold out there. I think my ears have frozen solid." He set the bags on the dresser while she locked up again behind him. His hands were red and so were his cheeks, chapped by the sharp wind that had sent her scurrying from car to room when they'd arrived.

"I can't promise how hot anything is after the run across the parking lot, but it smells good." In the process of unloading the bags, he noticed she was still standing by the door. "What?"

She shook her head and crossed to claim her food, taking it to her bed. She'd been thinking of all he'd done today—meeting her at, or at least near, the prison, giving her a ride, buying her first McDonald's hamburger in more than a year. Saving her from those men at the bus stop, taking her to Atlanta. Remembering that she liked onion rings and loved cocoa. It was more than anyone had done for her, or remembered about her, in twelve years, maybe twenty. It was enough to make her feel.

And she wasn't going to feel. He had his reasons. She couldn't let herself forget that. The fact that he'd remembered her preference for rings and cocoa was meaningless. It was probably detailed, along with all her other likes and dislikes, in a case file somewhere. No doubt, he'd reviewed it before heading for the prison today.

She sank on the bed, slowly unwrapping foil from the burger, a sense of wonder building inside her. Twelve hours ago, she'd been in prison, wearing her tacky uniform, sticking to the schedule they'd set for her, making a point of minding her own business. Now here she sat, long after lights-out, on a comfortable bed in a motel in east Texas, eating restaurant food way past dinnertime. Tonight there would be no talk to disturb her sleep, no snoring unless it was Dean's, no crying unless it was her own. She was a free woman.

Then her gaze shifted to Dean. *Free* being relative. Still, for sheer good looks and disposition, he beat her old cellmate by a mile. On a good day, LaRinda was about as charming as a snake and trustworthy as a troll, and she hadn't had many good days.

He took the other bed, food spread across sheets and drink on the night table. As he broke open a packet of salt to sprinkle on his fries, he asked, "How come you didn't learn to drive until you were twenty?"

She'd told him that, hadn't she? No matter. Surely his friends at the police department—all private investigators had them, didn't they?—could tell him that she'd been a late bloomer when it came to cars. "No car until then, no point in learning to drive."

"What about when you were sixteen? Didn't your parents have a car?"

Her father, she'd learned, had had a garage full of them. At fifteen, Miri had sold her mother's aged car with a forged signature to buy food and medication. The car was worthless to them. It didn't run half the time, and by then, Mom's mental condition had deteriorated to the point that she rarely left her bed.

"We took the bus when it was convenient and walked when it wasn't."

"This 'walking' you speak of…it's an alien concept." He scooped up some fries. "I got that car for my sixteenth birthday. Keep in mind, it didn't run, was missing all its glass and had only two tires and no doors, but it was the best gift I ever got. My dad and I worked on it every evening until it was like brand-new. Good times." Popping the fries into his mouth, he chewed and swallowed before asking, "Did you ever do anything like that with your dad or mom? You know, a mother-daughter project."

"Not unless forcing a pill she didn't want to take into her mouth, then holding her jaws shut until she swallowed counts," Miri murmured, then went utterly still. Oh, God, had she said that out loud?

She must have, because Dean was staring at her with—surprise? Shock? Pity? Her shoulders straightened. She didn't want pity, not from him or anyone else. She'd *loved* her mother. She'd committed seven years of her life to taking care of her, and she didn't regret or resent one minute of it.

Aggression built inside her, her muscles tightening, her

gaze narrowing as she waited for him to pursue the subject or, worse, say something totally inane like *I'm sorry.* But all he did was look at her a moment, then, casually, easily, he changed the subject as if he'd lost interest in the previous one.

"So what do you think of your first day without prison guards?"

Tension drained from her neck, her jaw, even her teeth. She breathed once, twice, something that felt like gratitude pumping through her veins. "Considering the company, it's not that different."

"Aw, come on, you gotta admit, I'm better looking than most of the guards, and I'm as strong as at least one or two."

An image comparing him to the female guards in her cellblock almost made her smile. "Maybe one or two. But most of them could take you in a fair fight, and there are a few who could probably bench-press you."

"Hey, it's hard to fight a woman. My dad taught me not to hit girls. My mom taught me not to hit anyone unless they hit me first."

Her mother had had the same rule: no nonsense about gender, just don't start a fight, but defend yourself if someone else did.

"From where I stood at the bus station, it was kind of hard to fight a man, too."

Dean feigned a wounded look as he gingerly touched his jaw. "The guy sucker punched me. I didn't even know he was there. How can you protect yourself against someone you don't even know is there? And you with the warnings…"

This time she did smile. It was rusty and unnatural but vaguely familiar. If she tried hard, she could remember a time when smiles came as easily to her as they did to Dean. If she got sentimental enough to make a Christmas wish, maybe it would be for the smiles to come back.

"All right, all right. Enough with the whining. The next time I'll yell, 'Dean, watch out!'"

Again he stared at her. For a moment she couldn't think why, then she realized: she'd said his name. A meaningless thing, but somehow, in a musty motel room with the television on Mute and the wind howling outside, it seemed intimate.

Awkwardly she shifted on the bed, tossing aside the burger she was finished with, fingering a lukewarm onion ring, gathering her defenses close again. "Besides," she muttered, "it isn't going to happen again."

"From your lips to God's and Santa's ears." He stood, held out his hand for her trash, then headed toward the wastebasket in the corner. Glancing back with a devilish grin, he added, "I'm too handsome to get a black eye for Christmas."

"Aw, doesn't it get you sympathy from the girls?"

"You wouldn't be sympathetic if my whole face was pounded into ground beef, and you're the only girl around right now." He yawned, stretching his arms high above his head, then picked up his duffel. "I'm gonna take a shower, then go to bed. I suppose you've already got the alarm set for presunrise."

"I don't need an alarm. The call to wake up in prison is not subtle. I'll never be able to sleep in again in my life."

He closed the door behind him, then the water came on. Swinging her feet to the floor, she sat on the bed and savored the last drops of the cocoa, which stirred way too many memories that she couldn't handle right now. After tossing the cup into the trash, she turned off the TV and the lights on her side of the room and slid into bed, facing the wall, covers heaped over until she was sure only a spot of her hair showed. Arms around Boo, she closed her eyes, slowed her breathing and slowly drifted off to sleep.

* * *

Dean knew the instant he reentered the room that Miri was asleep. That was how strong her personality, or their connection or whatever it was, was. Her breathing was steady where she curled around the bear, one hand holding tightly to him, the other cupped to her cheek. Hell, she looked about ten years old. When she really was ten, had she ever been allowed the freedom of childhood? How long had she been nursing a mother who didn't want to be nursed?

So far he'd learned that her mother had been ailing, she had at least two siblings, they'd had no car and had lived where snow and buses were common, and she'd made zero mention of a father. Had he never been around, or were there different dads for the kids? Or had her father been a rat-bastard who abandoned them because the responsibility was more than he'd wanted?

Dean had worked his share of deadbeat dad cases. He despised men who could live in new houses, buy new vehicles, take vacations and help support their current girlfriend's kids but couldn't spare a dime for their own children. If Miri's father was like that, no wonder she'd never mentioned him. And had trust issues. And a less-than-happy childhood.

He watched her a moment longer before the idea that he was violating her privacy made him turn away, stuffing clothes into a laundry bag, turning off lights and crawling into the other bed.

He was out cold in seconds, sleeping through the night and awakening to the country tune of a reindeer hit-and-run coming through the window, audible even over the sound of the big diesel engine warming up. Sliding out of bed, he walked to the window, lifting one corner of the blackout curtains to find a big white truck, not just a pickup but a monster-size dually, lights on, doors open, two men carrying bags from room to truck. They were dressed in camo-patterned jackets and hats with earflaps, and black scarves hid everything exposed but their eyes. Even through the scarves, puffs of air formed when they spoke, and the truck's exhaust was billowing out clouds of white.

"Damn, it looks cold," he muttered.

"Twenty-eight degrees with wind out of the west gusting to twenty-five miles per hour."

He let the flap fall and returned to his bed. "How do you know that?"

"I called the desk and asked after my shower." Miri sat up, and in the dim light he could see she was already dressed.

"You really did intend to get out before sunrise, didn't you?" He groaned for effect as he flopped back down on his bed.

"Check the clock. It's 8:15."

This time his groan was real. "Where's the snow?"

"Coming."

"Then we'd better get going."

By the time he'd changed clothes and brushed his teeth, she was standing near the door, wearing the blue coat over her black sweatshirt and the ball cap on her head. Her left arm was wrapped tightly around the bear. "You can wait here while I get the car warmed up," he said as he shoved the rest of his stuff into the duffel.

"I'd rather not."

One of his off-and-on rules for the business: pick his arguments. This wasn't important enough to count. Shrugging into his drastically insufficient leather jacket, even with a sweater under it, he shouldered the strap of his duffel, took her pack and led the way to the car. The white pickup was gone.

The air was so cold, it had substance, sliding over his bare hands and cheeks with edges sharp enough to cut. Every breath out froze and hovered, as if it might fall to the ground in shards, before finally drifting away. The sun might as well not exist, its thin rays unable to pierce even the tiniest of holes in the thick veil of gray cold, and the wind was adding its own torment.

He thought of his parents on that cruise ship in the Caribbean and would have wept if he weren't too macho for tears.

The metal of the car shrieked as they opened the doors, the leather seats creaking as they slid inside. The engine turned over on the first try, but it took a while to get warm air from the heater vents. "Breakfast inside or to go?" he asked as he drove around the motel corner and into view of the restaurant.

"To go." Miri snuggled closer to the bear. She was pale, her cheeks pink, her lips tinged with blue, probably colder than she'd ever been since those Christmases in the snow with her mom and siblings.

"I've gotta get gas." He pulled up to an empty pump, drew a breath and launched out into the cold. He'd known a front was blowing in when he'd packed yesterday, so why hadn't he grabbed gloves, scarves and hats? Why hadn't he taken the down-filled jacket that, true, had no style compared to the leather one but made subfreezing temperatures actually bearable?

His fingers were numb by the time he finished pumping gas. With a sigh of relief, he went inside the moist heat of the store and cruised the aisles before going to pay. He returned to the car balancing two large cups of coffee with three plastic bags, giving them to Miri to put away. "Breakfast is in one of the bags. But first grab those gloves and hats. There's a knife in the glove box to cut off the tags."

She opened one bag, filled with sweets, chips and bottles of water. From the second, she pulled out two pairs of black gloves, one large, one small, and two knitted caps, his black, hers pink. She cut the tags and, he would bet, didn't think he noticed that she slid the four-inch lockback into her pocket instead of returning it to the glove box.

He didn't mind if she was armed. He was reasonably confident she wouldn't use the knife on him. If he'd slept soundly enough for her to shower and dress without disturbing him, she likely could have found the pistol he'd tucked under the extra pillow. Though he'd prefer to think he wouldn't be oblivious to a beautiful woman rummaging in his bed....

She handed him gloves and the black hat, and he tugged the hat on as he pulled away from the pump. She pulled on her own hat, then flipped down the visor to get a look in the mirror. "Pink? Really?"

"It was that, lime-green or a Santa hat with flashing lights around the fur."

"Pink is fine." Pushing the visor back, she set the two bags in the backseat, then opened the third one. He'd grabbed two maple-frosted doughnuts, four sausage biscuits, two hash browns in greasy paper sleeves and two tortillas filled with scrambled eggs and sausage. "Hot food from a gas station? Do you have a death wish?"

"Hey, in some areas, gas-station food is as good as any restaurant. It's not like getting it from a vending machine or anything."

Predictably, after handing him a tortilla and a hash brown, she chose a doughnut for herself, practically moaning over the sugary-sweet flavor of the maple. Too intent on watching her, he almost rolled through a stop sign until a ground-shaking honk from a passing semi snapped him out of it.

"I love maple," she murmured, oblivious to his stare.

"Yeah, I remember." He remembered more than he wanted—and wished there had been more *to* remember.

Like how she looked naked. How she felt beneath him. How she woke up after a long night of not sleeping. Tousled, drowsy, soft, sweet...

"Did you hear anything in there about the weather?"

He checked both mirrors before accelerating on to the interstate, heading east and hopefully to warmer weather, growing friendliness and some clue where Mr. Smith's money was. "That was all I heard. 'Merry Christmas, Happy Holidays, there's snow fifty miles west.'"

"I hope it stays there." She finished the last bite of doughnut, licked the sugar from her fingers—*damn!*—then looked into the bag again. This time she chose a biscuit, folding back the paper, eyeing the bread and sausage cautiously before taking a small bite.

Dean concentrated on driving and eating until he was full and the coffee was cooled enough to drink. He glanced at Miri, fingers wrapped around her own coffee, and tried to inject casual interest into his voice. "Okay...Atlanta doesn't get many white Christmases, so that's not where you grew up. Maybe northern Georgia? There are mountains in that part, aren't there?"

"There are a few hills," she replied drily.

"Don't make fun of my geography knowledge. I can take you anywhere you want to go in the Dallas area blindfolded. But the only place I've been in Georgia is the Atlanta airport on my way to or from elsewhere." He paused. "You have family there?"

"At the Atlanta airport?"

"Miriam," he chided.

She looked at him briefly before turning her attention to her coffee, taking a long drink. He fully expected her to ignore him or tell him it was none of his business, but she surprised him. "Why don't you call me Miri?"

"Because I like Miriam. And I'm the only one who calls you that. Aren't I?"

"Yes."

"I suppose I could try to call you Miri if you insisted."

She gave him another look but didn't insist before reaching across to turn on the radio. A staticky "O, Holy Night" came from the speakers. She pushed the scan button and brought up "I'll Be Home for Christmas." After a few more tries with similar results, she punched the CD button and Trans-Siberian Orchestra's symphonic/heavy metal "Christmas Eve/Sarajevo 12/24" crashed out into the air. Scowling, she shut off the stereo. "What is it with you and Christmas music?"

"'Tis the season, and all that. Besides, I like it." He waited an extra beat before asking, "What is it with *you* and Christmas music?"

"It's just another day, one that millions of people don't celebrate. Do we have to be bombarded with all the hype?"

He turned on his blinker to switch lanes and pass a slow-moving dually, the same one from the motel, it looked like. Once he was back in the outside lane, he glanced at her. "Is that what Christmas is to you? Just another day? Hype? You said your mother loved Christmas."

"Yeah, well, she's dead, and I don't love it."

The words she snapped out and the way she stiffened as soon as she realized she'd said them both made his gut tighten. He couldn't imagine not having his mom around, especially during the holidays. Not that she was celebrating with the family this year, of course, but she was still celebrating, and everyone knew she would be home in a week and a half.

But to know she was gone, that there'd be no more decorating the house or singing carols or watching the Rudolph movie even if it did creep them out… No wonder Miri wasn't wild about the season.

The miles passed in a leaden gray blur. Middle of the day, and everyone's lights were on—headlamps, houses and businesses alongside the interstate, Christmas lights flashing on buildings and signs and even bales of hay in fields. The non-Christmas-celebrators couldn't catch a break, Miri thought with a scowl.

When the snow started, she tamped down a deep sigh. Watching it land on the windshield, the first flakes melting quickly before they slowly started to accumulate, the only thing she could think was—

"At least it isn't sleeting." Dean shifted, flexing his shoulders, then his fingers before switching on the wipers. "If it was ice, we'd have to pull over somewhere and wait it out. I couldn't risk this baby on ice." He gave the dash a comforting pat.

Miri snorted. "It wasn't even half a car when your parents gave it to you. Surely you could fix one more little ding."

His look feigned horror. "How about I rip that bear's arm off and give you a chance to sew it back on?" Without pausing for her response, he went on. "You don't 'ding' a treasure like this car. You don't even take chances on it."

"You drive in Dallas traffic every day. You park it in unattended lots. You take chances with it all the time."

He gave her a sidelong look, his mouth thinned. He'd taken the knitted cap off some miles back, when the car was warm enough, and his dark hair stood on end in places. It gave him a charming unpolished look. "You just don't understand the relationship between a man and his car."

She thought of her father and his cars. Any one of them would have supported her family for two years or more, and *his* baby, the big silver Bentley, could have kept them until they were grown. "Don't get it, don't want to."

He shook his head with chagrin. "How did I end up with a woman who refuses to recognize the importance of a vehicle in a man's life?"

Miri's first thought was to remind him—caustically— that he wasn't *with* her, not in any real sense. But some part that she'd thought had died from hopelessness and resignation twenty years ago wondered what it would be like to be *with* a man—and not just any man, but Dean. Would it be like her early years, when her mother was still healthy and her father had still loved them? There had been a lot of laughter then, a lot of kisses and a whole lot of "playing" in their room that she and Sophy, and later the younger kids, had been excluded from. They had sat side by side and held hands when they walked and snuggled on the couch.

In the ten-year run of the Smiths as a family, those times had been so much more common than the bad times, but Miri hardly ever remembered them. The bad times, the sad times, the crying times were so much stronger in her mind.

"What *do* you appreciate besides ragged old bears?"

She blinked rapidly to clear her eyes. Must be fatigue from staring at the snow without blinking. Definitely not tears. She hadn't cried since the day her mother had died.

But something had shorted in her brain, and she answered honestly. "Second chances." Didn't that sound like something a newly released felon should say? Quickly, before her nerve failed her, she went on. "You giving me this ride. I know you're hoping I'll lead you to the money, and that's not going to happen, but...I appreciate it just the same."

His gaze was steady enough to make hers waver. After a long moment, he said, "You're welcome."

Was she disappointed he hadn't denied wanting to recover the money for his client? A few sweet words from him about just seeing her safely to her destination would have felt good, for about as long as it took her to remember that all his sweet words and actions last year had just been part of his job.

No, she preferred honesty, even if his lack of denial did send a bit of regret shivering through her. She already had so many regrets—though not about taking the money. Her father owed them that, down to the last penny. Nothing she'd done to protect her mother or herself niggled at her conscience, either. They'd had to survive in a world that didn't offer much help, so she made no apologies.

She did regret the life she hadn't lived. Once Social Services had come around, she never had another real friend. She'd learned to not even open herself to the possibility. She'd kept everyone at an emotional distance, and when she was old enough, she'd fixated on finding Sophy, Oliver, Chloe and their father and getting the money he owed them.

And she regretted that the first person she'd chosen to trust since her mother's death had been Dean. Sweet, charming, sexy, stubborn Dean. She'd opened herself to that possibility, all right, and look what it had gotten her.

Learn from your mistakes. That had been a common refrain in prison.

Men were put here to break our hearts, baby. Mom's best advice.

She wouldn't start wanting anything sweet from Dean. She would prove she'd learned from that mistake.

Before she could decide exactly how she would prove it, Dean muttered, "Damn." She looked at him, then followed his tense gaze to the road. There was plenty of distance between him and the next vehicle—he was careful about that—but in front of it, traffic was slowing, brake lights flashing like a Christmas display gone wild. As she watched, far ahead a tractor-trailer jackknifed and slid as if in slow motion to block both lanes. She imagined she could hear the crumpling of metal and shattering of glass as the vehicles immediately behind it crashed into each other. At the same time she muttered a silent curse, Dean whispered a soft prayer.

He braked, three quick taps, and began to steer the car toward the shoulder. Her fingers knotting in Boo's fur, she glanced in the rearview mirror and gasped. "Dean!"

A white pickup was bearing down on them, the vehicle high enough off the ground that all she could see was grille and one headlight. Breath catching in her lungs, she whispered in her head—*please, please, please*—and waited for the collision, the force that would whip them forward within their seat belts, that would crumple the trunk and fenders and probably a good part of the car's interior if the damn giant truck didn't just roll over them like a dozer.

Dean jerked the wheel hard to the right, across the shoulder and into the grass, and the truck sailed past with no more than a few inches' clearance. The Charger skidded sideways a few feet before stopping near the edge of a culvert. As far as Miri could see, the occupants of the truck didn't even glance back, and the driver didn't stop to make sure they were all right.

The snow dampened the traffic sounds and collected in fragile blobs on the passenger windows while the wipers still worked to clear the windshield. Her breathing was audible over the rush of the heater, and suddenly she was so cold she couldn't register the warm air blowing over her.

"Are you okay?"

She breathed. "Yeah. More importantly, no dings on the car."

The sound he made was derisive. "Don't you love the Christmas spirit in all these good Samaritans stopping to see if we need help?"

"We didn't actually hit anything, and it's probably all they can do to concentrate on not winding up here themselves."

He gave her an incredulous look. "Miriam Scrooge defending the common holiday traveler?"

"I'm not a Scrooge." She paused a moment. "I prefer Grinch."

His chuckle had a startled quality to it, then the humor passed and he exhaled deeply, blowing out the tension of the past few minutes, she figured. If she'd been overcome with the sick fear that they were going to be in a wreck, he must have had double the anxiety for the danger to his car.

"There's an exit just up ahead. We're gonna have to get off the interstate at least for a while. It'll take 'em a long time to clean this up." Rolling down his window, he swiped the snow from the rearview mirror, looked, then slowly eased back on to the pavement. He didn't try to merge but stayed on the shoulder the few hundred yards to the exit.

The exit took them to a crossroad with two gas stations, one rundown diner and a shabby motel. Dean pulled into a parking lot. "Do you know where the atlas is?"

"I put it—" She reached into the backseat at the same time he did, bumping heads with him, looking up to find him far too close. For an instant, a moment, all they did was stare. His blue eyes were dark, grim, then slowly something else seeped in. *A memory,* she thought. A kiss. A taste. Heaven help her, *she* still remembered. If she wasn't careful, she could still want, still need—

Nothing sweet. Not from Dean.

The reminder should have made her straighten, putting as much space between them as possible. She should have let him know beyond a doubt that she wasn't interested in resurrecting *anything* with him. Once he delivered her to Atlanta, she would never see him again.

But she didn't straighten, didn't move away so much as a

breath. Her skin was hot, her fingers nerveless, her breathing shallow and as unsteady as the beat of her heart. *One small resurrection,* the sly voice inside her coaxed. *One kiss,* the loneliness inside her pleaded.

"Miriam." His voice was husky, her plain, nothing-special name sounding very special. His eyes darkened, and he moved closer, even though they were already intimately close. She thought he was going to kiss her and didn't know if she could be strong enough to push him away. She'd been the strong one her whole life, and just once, just for two minutes, she wanted someone else to take that role. Just once she wanted—

"I've got it," he murmured.

Got what?

Then he sat back, pulling the road atlas with him. A grin spread across his face, appealing for all its smugness. "You thought I was going to kiss you."

Heat flared, scorching her cheeks, as she resettled in her seat. Lord, if she opened the door, she could probably melt all the snow within a ten-foot radius. "I didn't—"

"I'm going to. Just not now. Not here."

Not now, not here, not ever. "You're pretty sure of yourself," she said with a sniff.

"It's on my Christmas wish list."

"Yeah, well, good luck with that."

"I don't need luck. Santa never disappoints those who truly believe, and I do."

And life never disappointed those who were smart enough not to believe. If she never hoped for anything, then she could never be disappointed.

But try as she might to pretend she'd run out of hope twelve years ago, she was kidding herself. She had high hopes for this visit with Sophy. She hoped Oliver and Chloe would welcome her back into their lives. She hoped some-

where in their hearts they remembered her and their mom.
She hoped she wouldn't have to spend the rest of her life
alone.

What was hoping for one little kiss compared to all of
that?

Chapter 4

Dean figured out an alternative route on state highways, hoping to get on the interstate at the next access some forty miles away. After stowing the map, this time between the driver's seat and the console, he dug in the rear seat again for a bottle of water and a bag of chips, then shifted into gear and pulled back onto the highway.

Thanks to the pileup on the interstate, the two-lane road had heavier traffic than was usual, but the increased volume kept the road pretty clear of snow, so he didn't have to concentrate totally on driving.

Which meant he could think about Miri and how good she smelled and how close they'd been. He should have kissed her while he'd had the chance. It had been a long time since he'd kissed anyone besides his mother.

Fifteen or sixteen months.

Since his last date with Miri.

He forced his fingers to loosen their grip on the steering

wheel as the realization settled in his gut. He'd gone out with a few women since her arrest, but he hadn't kissed even one of them. Hadn't thought about it. Sure as hell hadn't thought about having sex with them.

Of course, he'd been busy. The embezzlement hadn't been his only case, and after tying that up, it had been Christmas, then New Year's and old cases, new cases, life in general. It hadn't been any kind of obligation to Miri—or worse, commitment—that kept him celibate. Just some dates a man got lucky, some he didn't and some he didn't want to.

Deliberately he shifted to a safer course of thought. The dually that had almost hit them had been the same one he'd seen at the motel. Was it coincidence, or did it mean something?

The rational voice in his head said of course it meant something: that the vehicle had been traveling east on I-20 with them. That the men had stopped for the night at the motel, just like them. That they'd continued their trip in the same direction, just like him and Miri. It couldn't mean anything else. He hadn't told anyone he'd made contact with her or that he'd be traveling with her. His policy was to not bother clients with little details unless they insisted on it, and Mr. Smith didn't. He trusted Dean to do his job well without guidance.

Still, coincidences bothered him, even though life was full of them.

"You said three sisters and two husbands. Did one of your sisters get divorced?"

Miri's voice startled him. She was so good at being quiet that it took him a moment to grasp that she was actually initiating conversation. "Bette's in the process. Her husband ran off last summer with the nanny, who was all of twenty. I offered to fly up and smash his face in, but she settled for hiring the best divorce lawyer in Chicago instead."

"Good for her." After a pause, she added, "Lucky for you."

He scowled, but his heart wasn't in it. "The guy *sucker punched* me. You know, I've won most of the fights I've been in."

"You certainly won ours."

"What we had wasn't a fight, Miriam. It was a relationship."

"Until you brought the police to arrest me."

Something hot prickled along his neck. He wouldn't feel guilty about doing his job, damn it. "You said you didn't hold that against me."

"I don't. I just wish…"

After a moment's silence, he coaxed, "What? Tell Santa's helper and maybe, if you've been a good girl, he'll make it come true."

Her fingers worked the bear's fur, in contrast to the wry smile she gave him. "I was good enough for the Department of Corrections to let me go." Then she gave him a measuring look. "You're kind of big to be an elf, aren't you?"

"Not all of Santa's helpers are elves." His grin was as good-natured as he could make it. "I've never put on tights and curly-toed shoes, but my sisters bullied me into donning the red suit and beard a couple of times. Scared the hell out of my nieces and nephews. I swear, the baby girls recognized my scent or something because to this day, those two are wary around me."

"Smart girls."

"The other five girls and the two boys love me," he protested, slowing to follow the line of cars ahead of them onto a northbound road. If he'd read the map correctly, this road would eventually turn east and lead them right back to the interstate. Or he could just follow the other drivers.

"Your family's really heavy on the girl gene, aren't they?"

"Yeah, but I'm planning on having at least a couple of boys. No matter how many girls it takes to get them."

"You have someone in mind for doing the actual *having?*"

It was stupid and juvenile, but the image that popped into his head immediately was Miri, surrounded by little boys, all black-haired and blue-eyed like him and beautiful like her. Tough like her, too. And, of course, charming like him.

When he didn't answer, she laughed drily. "Yeah, it's kind of hard to have that kind of relationship when you start out the first date with the multiple-babies/boys thing, isn't it?"

Consider yourself warned, he thought, then wasn't sure if he was talking to himself or her.

The squeak of the wipers drew his attention to the fact that the snow had stopped. He turned them to the low setting to keep the windshield clean of splashing from the traffic before asking, "What about your family? All girls or mostly boys?"

Apparently in sudden need of a lukewarm drink, she leaned into the back for a bottle of water and a candy bar. When she'd taken a swig, she tore open the plastic wrapper on the candy but didn't take a bite. "Three girls, one boy."

Wow, more information that I didn't have to pry out with a crowbar. It's my lucky day, considering my car almost ended up in a ditch. "Let me guess. You're the oldest."

"I am."

"What about their kids?"

The look that crossed her face showed him the true meaning of *bittersweet.* It was haunting and sad and full of love and sorrow, and it made him want to wrap his arms around her and make everything all right, at least for the moment.

"I don't know. I haven't been in touch with them for a long time."

Long was relative. A couple of years? Five? Ten? Had she left home at the first chance she'd gotten? Had her parents kicked her out? Had she done something to cause them to break off contact with her? Not likely, if she'd been caring for her sick mother.

But the mother had died. Maybe Miri had no longer felt needed. Maybe things had been bad between her and her father. Maybe the grief had driven her to someplace new.

There was so much he didn't know about her. So much he wanted to know.

"Sorry." It was a meaningless word that made him wish for something else to say, but if the right thing was in his brain, he couldn't locate it.

"Yeah, well, you know what they say. Stuff happens."

He grinned again. "You must not be from Texas, because around here, we don't say 'stuff.'" He hesitated. Another personal question might make her shut up again, but she'd started it, right? And he doubted she would volunteer much, if anything, without his asking. "Where are you from?"

The wipers swiped slowly left, back to the right, then left again before a small shiver rippled through her. "North Carolina."

His breathing automatically grew shallow, as if a full inhalation might startle her. "You don't sound like a Tar Heel." Though accents could be lost, learned or faked. He knew that from work experience.

"I left there a long time ago."

Long again. Relative, again. "You're only thirty. How long could it have been?"

His breathing might be shallow. Hers was heavy and weary. "Twelve years. And enough with the questions."

She'd left home at eighteen, most likely on her own. What had happened to her sisters and brother? Did they wonder where their big sister had gone? Did they care? Did they even remember her?

That desire to hold her tight intensified, but he settled

for gripping the steering wheel. If he tried to touch her, she would probably withdraw, because no matter what she said, she did blame him for her arrest.

He understood that. He just wished she understood that he hadn't had a choice. It just wasn't in him to ignore a crime. His duty to Mr. Smith and his own sense of honor had required him to do the right thing.

But if they'd met under different circumstances, if Mr. Smith had never hired him or she'd never been tempted by her boss's fortune...

Maybe that should go on his Christmas wish list, but changing the past was impossible, even for the big guy with the elves.

"So how do we talk if I can't ask questions?"

Her eyes narrowed, fine lines wrinkling her forehead. "We don't have to talk. We could just be quiet and enjoy the scenery."

"What scenery? It's gray, dreary, the snow is turning to slush, my car's getting dirty and we're following a bunch of other dirty cars."

"We're not sitting on the side of the road waiting for state troopers and wreckers while you whine over the damage to your precious car."

"Yeah. Good point." He tried to be quiet. He really did. But that just wasn't in him either. Not even six minutes had passed, according to his watch, before he asked, "Are you going to North Carolina after we get to Atlanta?"

She finally took a bite of the candy bar she'd torn open earlier, more to delay responding than from hunger, he'd bet. After swallowing that, she rested the stuffed bear on her feet, then shrugged out of her coat and tossed it into the backseat, picked up the bear again and—finally—answered with a question of her own. "It's not the keep-having-babies-until-you-get-boys thing that's keeping you single, is it?

You just talk until women run away screaming, desperate for some quiet."

"I can make women scream. But trust me, Miriam—" he smiled smugly "—it's got nothing to do with talking."

I'm not a screamer.

Miri kept the retort inside—knowing Dean, he'd take it as a challenge and, knowing herself, he'd prove her wrong— and, with exaggerated patience, answered one more of his questions. "No, I'm not going to North Carolina." *Yet.* "Where I am going has nothing to do with the money." *Liar.* "What I am planning to do at this moment is take a nap. Is that allowed?"

His expression was petulant—put-on, she suspected, like a lot of his arrogance. Not to say that he didn't come by his smugness naturally. Just that he was overdoing it. She couldn't help but wonder why.

"How can you need a nap? You slept like a baby last night."

"How can you know that? You slept like a rock."

His gaze flashed to her, pleasure making his baby blues sparkle. "You watched me sleep?"

Not "watched." She just happened to have been lying on her right side when she woke up, and he just happened to be in her line of sight, and the bathroom light he'd left on just happened to cast its dim glow on him.

And not for long. Only long enough to want…

She was a grown, healthy woman who'd spent all but one of the past 433 days locked up with other women. She'd had sex. She'd liked it. It was only natural to want to have it again, though not necessarily with Dean. It was simply that he was the only man around, except for those two jerks at the bus station, and she most certainly didn't want to have sex with two jerk strangers.

Did that mean Dean wasn't a jerk? Or merely that he wasn't a stranger?

She held up Boo and gestured toward the side window. "Can I take a nap?"

His reply was grudgingly given. "Yeah." Then he tossed the black cap from the dash to her. "You might want to put this between it and the window so the condensation doesn't get it wet."

How sad was her life that his minor consideration for Boo touched her somewhere inside?

She tugged the cap over Boo's head, completely covering his face, then rested the bear against the window and her head against the bear. The cap smelled of shampoo and... Surreptitiously she breathed deeper, but there was nothing else to smell.

Oh, she was even sadder than she'd thought, disappointed that a recently purchased hat Dean had worn for maybe thirty whole minutes didn't retain some scent of him.

"What's that thing stuffed with? I can hear it all the way over here."

She closed her eyes and pretended to relax. "A lot of toy animals have stuffing that crinkles so the child can make noise with it. Besides, if you were as old as Boo, you'd be a little creaky, too."

"I'm feeling older by the minute," he murmured, but with every intention of her hearing.

She didn't actually mean to go to sleep. Given the circumstances, she'd slept fairly well the night before. But the rhythmic *whick* of tires on pavement lulled her away. *Just for a minute.* But the next thing she recognized was the absence of that sound.

She opened her eyes, but one saw only blackness. Dean's cap, she remembered groggily. Her face was smushed against Boo, no doubt leaving the weave's imprint on the right side and making for a less than attractive squishiness on the left side. Raising her head, she yawned broadly, then looked around. "Where are we?"

"The bright metropolis of Sunshine, Mississippi."

"No, really, where are we?"

"Really, Sunshine. See?" He pointed to a faded yellow sign listing to the sun-setting position above the entrance to a convenience store. "Population, fifty or so, I'd guess, plus a pack of mangy cats." They were gathered at the Dumpster beside the store.

"Why are we stopping?"

"One, we need gas. Two, I'm hungry. And three, I really need to take a—" He broke off when she scowled at him. "Look, there's the bright spot in this town. Fat Boy's Fried Chicken Hut. If that's not a name that draws you in, I don't know what is."

She gazed from him to the restaurant, not the most encouraging sight she'd ever seen. Small, drab, definitely not a five-star place, but the Shell parking lot was filled with vehicles, most with Mississippi plates. The locals seemed to like it, and if a fat Southern boy didn't know his fried chicken, who did?

They parked with a half dozen other cars on a patch of yellowed grass, and Dean climbed out, stretching his arms high over his head, enough to give her a glimpse of his flat, ridged stomach before he tugged his sweater back down. It had been so long since she'd seen the sexy parts of any man, much less touched, and damn it, she was still a sucker for rock-hard abs.

Maybe still a bit of a sucker for him.

He bent to see through the door. "You coming?"

"Yeah. Sure." But after opening her own door, she hesitated. Since recovering Boo from the storage locker, he hadn't been more than a foot from her, and she hated to let this be the first time. What if someone stole Dean's car while they were inside?

The chilly breeze tousling his hair, he grinned. "When Cathy didn't give up her security blanket by the time she started school, my mother cut off a little square so she could stick it in her pocket. Want me to cut off his arm or an ear for you?"

Her scowl was only half-pretend. "What about yours? Did your mom cut off a piece of it, too?"

"She did. I'll show it to you sometime. Bring it if you want, or you can stick it in the trunk. Just decide. I'm cold and hungry and I still need to take a—" He broke off with a shrug and shoved his hands into his gloves.

It was hard, but she placed Boo carefully on the backseat, then covered him with plastic shopping bags. She slid out of the car and into her jacket, then hustled to follow Dean into the restaurant.

The heat inside fogged the windows, painted with manger scenes and majestic gold stars, and the aroma when they'd taken three steps was enough to make her mouth water. She hadn't had really good fried chicken since her mother had been well enough to fry it herself, with mashed potatoes and cream gravy, biscuits, stewed greens and fried okra, and pecan pie for dessert. *So* long ago, before the state had taken the other kids. *Too much trouble for just two,* she'd said after that, but Miri had known the truth. Too many memories, too much sorrow.

They found a table in the middle of the room and ordered the lunch special—no greens, but otherwise the same menu she remembered—with sweetened mint tea that was sensory overload all by itself. After a sip that made her sigh with appreciation, she said, "So your names are Adele, Bette, Cathy and Dean. I guess your father was willing to take as many girls as he had to, to get a boy? No need for an Elizabeth, Ellen or Esther after you?"

"Nah. They agreed on four from the start, though my dad always said they had me so the girls wouldn't pester them." His grin made it clear who pestered whom. "What are your names? Miriam and who else?"

It wouldn't hurt to answer. It would take more work to connect Miriam Duncan to Sophia Marchand, Oliver Baxter and Chloe Carson than Dean would ever want to do. Besides, first he would have to connect Miriam Jane Duncan to Alicia Miriam Smith, and the odds of that were slim to nothing. So she told him.

"Old-fashioned names."

"Old-fashioned mother."

"And your father?"

Selfish. Disinterested. Coldhearted. SOB. "Ran out on us when Chloe was three. Never came back." Her attempt at a careless smile was a miserable failure, just like her father had been.

"You haven't seen him since?"

She shrugged. She'd seen the man, but he wasn't her father anymore. Now that she had the money he'd owed them, he was nothing to her. Not even worth hating.

"Want me to find him so you can tell him what you think of him?"

This time her smile was more genuine. "No, thanks. He doesn't care, and finally, neither do I."

She realized she actually meant it. The money wouldn't make up for his abandonment, for leaving his young children in the care of an emotionally unstable mother without so much as a dime of support. It wouldn't erase the fact that because of him, their mom had lost the kids and, eventually, her parental rights to the younger three, and it wouldn't make those eight years of Miri's life when she'd been the mom to the parent go away.

But the money had mattered to *him,* more than his wife and kids ever had, and that knowledge satisfied her.

Beyond that, John W. Smith was dead to her. She'd done her sentence in prison, and she was ready to start a new life. Maybe she would go back to being Ali again. Maybe she would trust a few people. Maybe even love one or two.

But not Dean. Lord, please not him. He'd already let her down once. She didn't know if she could survive it again.

When they left Fat Boy's, Dean was so full of good ole country cooking that all he wanted to do was stretch out somewhere quiet and warm and be lazy for three or four hours. But his car wasn't built for stretching out, and he didn't think Miri would be quiet if he made her sit in the front seat while he lazed.

They drove over the pavement on to the roadway, went a couple hundred yards and turned into the gas station. "You need anything while we're here?"

She shook her head, but when he got out of the car, so did she. At his glance, she gestured across the parking lot to a faint trail in the pine forest that led to a barely visible house on the other side. "I'm just going to walk a bit."

He studied her a moment, and she looked back evenly. He figured she'd long since accepted the fact that she was stuck with him for another day, and he *knew* she'd be back, because her bear was still in the backseat.

Ugly, ratty bear must have some damn good memories attached.

When he didn't say anything, she turned and started toward the trail with long strides. He didn't blame her for wanting exercise, even as cold as it was. He was a little antsy from spending so much time in the car himself. He didn't blame her for wanting fresh air, either, with no high fences, walls and guards around to watch her. Prison must have been tough.

Just not as tough as she was, he admitted with a smile.

The tank full, he was replacing the gas nozzle when tires squealed on the road. He glanced at the car, an old beat-up Chevy, then looked back down, twisting the gas cap tightly. He hadn't wanted the smell of fuel on his gloves, but the nozzle and the wind had damn near frozen his fingers.

He was opening the door to the store when shots rang out: one, a pause, another, a pause, one more, followed by the roar of a powerful engine and the screech of tires. *Miri!*

"Was that gun—"

Letting the door close on the clerk's question, Dean ran across the lot. He was dimly aware of voices behind him, of other footsteps, but he focused on the woods and the patch of blue crumpled on the ground next to a tree. His heart thudded in his chest and echoed in his ears, his lungs too tight to supply adequate oxygen, but as he neared, he managed enough to shout her name. "Miriam!"

A flash of pink appeared as she moved her arms from over her head, then her face, pale, brown eyes wide and stark. Before she had a chance to move any farther, he skidded to a stop beside her and grabbed her shoulders. "Are you okay? Are you hurt?"

Her hands clenched fistfuls of his sweater. "N-no, I'm o-okay."

He lifted her to her feet, then wrapped his arms around her, holding her so tightly he could feel the adrenaline buzzing through her, the trembling of the fear. "Oh, my God, I thought—" He wouldn't give voice to it. He couldn't.

"Everything all right here, son?" The deep voice came from behind him, and he looked up to see a handful of men, one of them wearing a badge pinned to his jacket. Having

the local cop in the convenience store at the time of a shooting... Talk about luck.

Then, as Miri's shivers subsided, he knew the luck was
that she hadn't been hurt. Or maybe it was more than luck.
This close to Christmas, who knew?

"Look at that," the clerk said, rubbing the damaged bark
of the tree. "Couldn't have missed her by more than a couple inches."

"Liquor improves his aim. If the moron had been sober,
he would've been off by a mile," a third man added.

Dean looked sharply at them. "You know who it was?"

The sheriff grimaced. "The car looked like T-Bone's.
He's not a bad ole boy. Just loses what little sense he has
when he's been drinking."

T-Bone. A local moron. Not one of Mr. Smith's hired
morons.

"He wasn't shootin' at you, ma'am," the clerk said, as
if that made a difference. "Him and his buddies just get a
little too much 'shine in 'em and does somethin' stupid."

Miri shifted to stand beside Dean, so his right arm remained around her shoulders, but she didn't move away
from him. "I understand moonshine does that to a person."
The dryness of her comment was undermined by the un-
steadiness of her voice.

"I'll go and talk to him," the sheriff went on. "Take his
gun away. Maybe let him spend a couple nights in jail. I
noticed you have Texas tags. You be able to come back for
court?"

"Yes," Dean said at the same time Miri replied, "No. I
won't be back this way again. Just do what you think best,
Sheriff. Put a little fear into him, maybe."

"We'll have a come-to-Jesus meeting he won't forget,
ma'am." The sheriff tipped his head. "If you'll come inside the store, I'll get some information from you for the

report. And I'm sure Judd here will be more than happy to collect the cost of your gas from T-Bone. It's the least the boy can do."

As the men headed back to the store, Dean felt a little wobbly in the knees. If Miri had been hurt... If he'd lost her...

His fingers convulsed until she winced, and he jerkily eased the pressure. "Sorry," he murmured.

She spared a small smile for him before turning to look at the gash on the tree. "Merry Christmas to me," she murmured.

Gently he bumped against her. "I'd sure hate to see you get shot on your first full day out of prison."

"I'd hate to get shot, period, especially by some goober who thinks 'shine and guns go together and answers to the name of T-Bone." She took a deep breath. "Though I wouldn't mind a little buzz myself about now."

"Maybe Judd will throw a six-pack of beer in with the gas." Dean took his own deep breath, rich with pine, his cologne and the sweet soapy scent still lingering from her morning shower. "Miriam—"

She looked up at him, and the words got caught somewhere in his throat. Instead of searching for them, he bent his head to hers and kissed her.

She didn't give him much time—just enough for a sweet taste, just enough for every part of his body to turn rock hard—before she pulled away. "Please don't," she whispered as she backed off to put space between them. She looked scared and hurt and like she'd wanted more, too. He'd caused both the fear and the hurt, but he could make it up to her if she just gave him a chance.

"Jeez, Miriam, I couldn't have done anything differently." He sounded hoarse and practically pleading, even to himself. "Can't you understand that? You broke the law. If you'd just been willing to give back the money, maybe I could have convinced Mr. Smith not to prosecute, but—"

Stiffly she backed away farther, all those emotions leaving her face as blank and cool as when she'd first recognized him outside the prison. "I told you, I don't blame you for that. I knew the risk I was taking."

Don't blame you for that. She sounded sincere, as if she really meant the words, which just confused the hell out of him. "Then what *are* you pissed about?"

Her head tilted to one side, her eyes narrowing to scrutinize him as if he were a bug under a magnifying glass—a glass she hoped was powerful enough to roast him alive. Then, as if what she saw disappointed her, she shook her head. "You really don't get it, do you? You lied to me. You used me. You tried to seduce me to get what you wanted. You made me think—" She bit off the words, spun around and headed back along the path to the station.

"Oh, no. Not this time." His strides easily surpassed hers so he could block her way. When she would have spun off again, he caught her hand. Even through her gloves, he felt tension streaking through her at the contact. "Made you think what?"

Her mouth thinned into the kind of look his mother used to give him when he'd broken all the house rules in one day. The better choice with a look like that was to release her, provided she didn't make another attempt at escape, so he did.

"I made you think what?" he repeated, using the kind of response-demanding tone his mother used.

Miri folded her arms over her chest and glared at him.

Okay, he was a private detective, so he would detect. She said he'd lied to her. True, but only in the course of his job. That he'd used her—not true—and tried to seduce her. Yeah, okay, not getting her into bed was one of his regrets. That he'd made her think…he wanted her? He cared about her?

He mimicked her position and her glare. "You think it was all part of the job? That the only reason I pursued you was to help with the case? For God's sake, Miri." He muttered a curse that wouldn't win him any points this close to Christmas, then moved closer, until he had to duck his head to continue glaring. "I don't get involved with women who are part of the job. I had no clue who was stealing Mr. Smith's money. I saw you in the office that first time, and I wanted to get to know you. I wanted to seduce you, sure, because you're beautiful and I'm a man, but mostly I just *wanted*. You.

"It had nothing to do with the case. Hell, I was thinking Trish Lewis was good for the embezzlement right up until the very end when I realized—" When it had just suddenly become clear to him. The thefts led back to their department. He was right about that much. But not to Trish. To Miri, whom he'd started falling for the first time he met her.

Falling for. Was that a clueless-guy term for falling in love? Had he been so focused on his work that he hadn't even recognized his own feelings? *Had* he been in love with Miri?

It would explain why he'd missed her so much. Why he hadn't found much satisfaction in closing out the Smith case. Why he hadn't had a serious date—or, more to the point, sex—since his last date with her. Why he'd been so eager to take Mr. Smith's offer that would put him right back into contact with her.

"—think that?" Indignation shone on Miri's face as she scowled up at him.

He shook his head, hoping to loosen a bit of those keen abilities that had kept him in business so long. "Sorry. I was thinking. What was that?"

"How could you possibly think Trish was stealing from her boss? She's a nice, honest, decent woman."

"How could I think *you* were doing it? You were nice, honest, decent, and I—I cared a lot about you. And yet you *were* stealing from your boss." It wasn't the right time or the place, but he touched her cheek. "Why, Miriam? He paid you well. You didn't need the money. If you've spent it, it hasn't been on yourself. You're not the criminal type. I bet you'd never stolen anything else before or after. So why did you do it?"

For just a second, she pressed against his hand—or maybe he imagined it, because the next second, she was shifting uneasily and avoiding his gaze. He was generally good at reading people. Some part of her wanted to answer, and another part wanted to dismiss both him and his questions. Finally she shrugged, dislodging his hand in the process, and flippantly said, "Let's just call it something I had to do. We should go. T-Bone's had time to break out another jar of 'shine, and if he comes back, all I'm likely to get for Christmas is dead."

She squeezed past him on the narrow trail, leaving Dean no choice but to follow.

He would get her talking again. Every piece of information she gave got him just a little closer to figuring her out, and once he'd done that, maybe he could persuade her to give back the money if she still had it. She could have the finder's fee, not much of a consolation prize for giving up more than a million bucks, but it came with him. Based on what she'd said a few minutes ago, he was pretty sure he was worth something to her.

Just maybe not enough.

Chapter 5

For God's sake, Miri.

He'd called her by her nickname. First time ever that he'd used it within her hearing, and it had sounded…nice. Maybe she would stick with Miri instead of going back to Ali, after all.

She sighed softly as she tried to find a more comfortable position. It had been a long day. She'd shared a room with Dean the night before, the pickup had run them off the road and some idiot had used her for celebratory target practice. The sun had never broken through the thick gray sky, the temperature had stayed steady in the too-damn-cold-for-the-South range and Dean had been unusually quiet since they'd driven away from Sunshine.

She wished he'd start talking again.

Like magic, her wish was granted. "We're almost there. Any particular area you want to stay?"

"No. You choose." Miri swallowed. As anxious as she'd

been to get to Atlanta, the closer they got, the more her stomach tightened, and since they'd crossed the state line, she'd had to focus on something, anything else to keep the queasiness at bay. Once she was in the city, her goal would be such a short drive away. Whether she found a ride to Copper Lake or Sophy chose to meet her in Atlanta, she would soon know how her future was going to unfold, good, bad or ugly.

She wasn't even sure what scared her most: Sophy rejecting her or accepting her back into her life.

Or saying a final goodbye to Dean.

I cared a lot about you. His words were the something else she'd been focusing on all afternoon. *I wanted to get to know you. But mostly I just wanted. You.*

She had believed that back then. Could she believe it now? He hadn't tried to contact her after her arrest. The prison had telephones; the inmates were allowed both mail and visitors. He'd shown up yesterday because of the money. But could there have been a secondary reason? Could he still care? Still want her?

It was safer not to believe him. If she didn't have hopes, then she couldn't be disappointed.

She'd spent twelve years keeping herself safe from emotional entanglements, and what had it gotten her? She was afraid of trying to give nearly three hundred thousand dollars—child support plus interest—to her own sister who had once loved her dearly. She was terrified of not being wanted.

She'd wanted to be wanted since she was ten years old, when she'd found out the state was giving her sisters and brother to other parents, when she'd learned that while her mother loved her, she wasn't enough to make up for the absence of the other three.

If what you've been doing isn't working for you, then it's time to try something new. Advice picked up from a counselor in prison. But she'd had her heart broken in one way or another by every member of her family and Dean. Could she trust him not to do it again? Could she trust any of them?

A half hour later, when he pulled into a motel parking lot, she still didn't know the answer.

As luck would have it, he'd left the interstate in a less-than-welcoming neighborhood. The first four places, right off the highway, were full of Christmas travelers. At the fifth, a far-from-its-prime motel about a mile from I-20, Dean returned from the office with a key and a skeptical look. "Good thing I have my gun."

Though she'd never touched a gun in her life, she might feel better if he'd brought an extra one for her. She would have to settle for the knife she'd taken from the glove box and slipped into her pocket. "At least they don't rent by the hour." Hopefully, she added, "Do they?"

"Nope. But I bet they double their rates when the nicer places fill up." He looked toward a strip of fast-food places, tucked between neon-lit bars, along the street. "See anything you like, or do you want to go find someplace?"

"How about ordering in pizza?" She'd noticed the sign for her favorite pizza chain while they'd been looking for a room.

"Sounds good."

He pulled around to park in front of a room in the center portion of the U-shaped building. The rooms on either side of theirs were dark, and she hoped it meant no one had rented them yet. Even from the parking lot, they heard TV shows from a few doors down in each direction. At least the place was only one story, so they wouldn't have upstairs neighbors to contribute to the noise.

The room was about what she expected—used well, cared for not so much. But she'd lived in worse places, the white sheets on the bed had been bleached to within an inch of their fibers shredding, and the bathroom was clean. What more did they need?

Dean wasn't quite so accepting. "Do you want to keep looking? There's got to be something better somewhere."

"This is fine. The heater works. The door locks." She sat down on one bed and gave an experimental bounce. "The bed's comfy. I'm tired. It's fine." If *tired* could also mean *a coward*.

He shrugged and set his bag on the other bed. He pulled the phone book from the shelf of the tiny night table, looked up the pizza place and started dialing. "Vegetarian, thin crust?"

"Yeah." Funny, the things he remembered. "Meat lovers, thick crust with extra cheese?"

His features formed sort of a smile before returning to exhaustion. "Yeah. One of my rewards for running regularly. Pizza, steak, ice cream..."

He placed the pizza order, then returned to the car to get the bag of bottled water and snacks he'd bought that morning. Uncapping a bottle, he took a long drink to swallow a couple of tablets he must have gotten from the car before sitting on the bed again. All they could do was wait for the delivery guy.

Miri lasted about five minutes in the silence. "I owe you a bunch of money."

Dean opened one eye. "Yeah. We'll settle up later."

"I'm good for it."

"I know. About three thousand times over." He stuffed a pillow behind him, then opened both eyes. "One computer genius to another, where'd you stash it? I got lost in all the transfers. Couldn't track the final ones."

"Someplace safe." Everyone had thought the money was still in overseas bank accounts. No one had suspected that she'd converted it to cash and hidden it in four storage lockers in Texas and surrounding states. That way, if one locker had been connected to her, she would only have lost one fourth of the money. *Her* fourth. No matter what, Sophy, Oliver and Chloe would have gotten their shares.

"Where'd you learn your computer skills?"

"Hacker friends."

"I didn't know you had friends."

The comment stung, though it was more true than he knew. Even before her mother's death, she'd known computers were the ticket to finding the rest of her family. She'd hooked up with a group of kids, outcasts like her, misfits, except her misfits had serious computer know-how. They hadn't really been friends—no one would have given her a second thought if she'd disappeared right in front of them—but they'd liked sharing their knowledge, and she'd soaked it in like a sponge.

"You want to go back to Dallas, I'll give you a job."

"A convicted felon?"

"Who's better with computers than I'll ever be. Use your powers for good."

The thought intrigued her—not working for Dean, but just working. Having a normal life without an agenda, not keeping secrets, being just a regular person. She hadn't given much thought to what she would do after she'd delivered the money to her sisters and brother. If they wanted her around, if they didn't—too scary to contemplate for long.

She did have skills, though, and she would need a job. Two-hundred-seventy-five-thousand dollars wouldn't support her forever. Besides, she didn't really *want* her father's money. Mostly she'd wanted him to *not* have it. It was a just debt that he'd refused to pay, so she'd given him no choice.

"Thanks, but I'm done with Texas. I'm not going back."

His eyes darkened, his expression turning grim. "Where are you going? You have to live somewhere."

"I don't know. I'll figure it out." *Somewhere I'm welcome.* Whether that would be near her family…she'd know tomorrow. December twenty-third. The day before the night before Christmas.

"How are you going to get wherever you're going?"

"I don't know that, either." Maybe take a bus, though she wouldn't hang out at the terminal this time, or if she did, she would stay close to the other passengers. Maybe she would hire a cab driver to take her all the way. For a tip double the fare, surely someone would be willing.

Or maybe you'll call Sophy. Give her a chance to tell you on the phone that she doesn't want to see you. She has her own family now, one who wanted her, one who chose her. No one chose you, Ali.

Miri tuned out the voice in her head, aided by the perfect timing of the delivery guy, rapping at the door, calling, "Pizza!" Dean paid him, then passed the smaller, steaming-hot box to her, along with a bottle of water, before sitting on the bed with his own medium pizza and water.

"You should rethink my offer," Dean said after finishing the first slice. "Let me take you all the way."

"No, thanks." She was prepared to say goodbye to him tomorrow morning, to stand at the door and watch as he drove out of sight, on his way back to Dallas. Delaying that goodbye by even so much as two hours would make it harder. Besides, she was also prepared to face Sophy the way she faced everything: alone.

"What if something happens?" he challenged.

"Like what?"

He rolled his eyes. "Like some perv trying to kidnap you at the bus station. Some jerk running you off the road. Some drunk taking potshots at you from his car."

"Coincidences. Bad luck. What are the odds of something bad happening again?"

"What are the odds of three bad things happening in less than twenty-four hours like that?"

She paused in the act of picking up another slice. "You think they weren't coincidences?"

Lines creased his forehead as he held her gaze. After a moment, he grudgingly said, "I don't know. T-Bone apparently has a history of shooting at things when he's drunk, and the men at the bus station might make a habit of hassling women anywhere they find them alone."

"And the men in the truck were just in a hurry to get where they were going." And Dean had a stake in sticking close to her. He couldn't recover the money if he didn't. "So I've used up my share of bad luck for at least a few days. I'll be fine. I don't need you to protect me."

She thought the subject was closed, but she was wrong. He was scowling so hard that she barely heard the words he muttered in response.

"Maybe you don't. But I need to know you're safe."

How could she be safe continuing to travel with him when the biggest danger she faced at that moment was him?

Coincidences. Bad luck. The words hummed through Dean's head while they ate, while Miri brushed her teeth and changed into her pajamas, while he brushed his own teeth and stripped down to his boxers and crawled into bed. He didn't like coincidences or bad luck, but obviously both happened. Was it possible the three incidents had been more than that?

The attempted kidnapping at the bus station absolutely could have been Bud Garvin's doing. He must have suspected, just like Dean, that Miri's first act out of prison would be to get the hell out of Texas, and her best way to do that was public transportation. Rental car agencies would have been hard to cover, but she'd never had a credit card, which most of them required these days. So Garvin would have also had people watching for her at the airports and the train stations.

The men in the pickup that ran them off the road could have been Garvin's people, too. He hadn't seen their faces, but size-wise, they seemed a close match to the men at the terminal. He hadn't noticed anyone following them to his place or on to the interstate, but with just about every other pickup on the road a white one, it was entirely possible.

T-Bone just didn't fit in. Even if the guys in the truck had followed them, they couldn't have known he and Miri would stop in that particular town for lunch. They couldn't have breezed in and found a local stupid enough to shoot at her in the ninety minutes they'd been there. Hell, after that accident on the interstate, they should have lost complete track of him and Miri.

And what was the point of having someone shoot at her? The job was recovering the money she'd stolen. A dead woman couldn't give that back. If they'd just wanted to scare her, why? Odds of her running back to Dallas to return the cash were somewhere between slim and none. A frightened woman would go into hiding—an easy thing to do on someone else's dime.

He'd already had a headache when they stopped for the night, and thinking in circles wasn't helping any. When he tried to stop, the next subject his mind went to was tomorrow morning and letting Miri go. No matter their agreement, could he really let her walk away from him? Could he return to Dallas without seeing her to her destination? Could he live not knowing where she was, if she was safe, if she needed him?

I don't need you to protect me, she'd said, and he was pretty sure she'd meant it. But he needed to know she was all right. He needed to be able to check on her. He needed to stay in touch with her so that if one day she might consider forgiving him, he could be there to help her along.

He had a lot of needs where she was concerned.

And the ten percent finder's fee was nowhere on the list, he was surprised to realize.

"Are you awake?" Her voice was soft, sweet, sexy.

"Yeah." He rolled onto his side to face her. Her hair gleamed golden in the thin light from the bathroom, but her face was nothing more than a pale oval, features indistinguishable.

She sat up, knees bent, arms resting on the covers over them. "If you had gone to your sister's house, what would you be doing now?"

It was an easy question. No matter where the Montgomerys met for Christmas, they had the same traditions. "They like to go caroling in the neighborhood and drive around to look at the Christmas lights, and the kids always have rehearsals for their church Christmas program. All of my sisters are bakers. They do thousands of cookies in the week before Christmas, and the kids deliver them to the neighbors. And shopping. The whole family are master shoppers."

She was quiet a long time. When she did speak, her tone was matter-of-fact, no emotion in it at all. "My last Christmas, we got new bikes, a trampoline, a basketball hoop and a lot of books. Mom thought kids should read to enrich their minds and play outside to exercise their bodies and their imaginations. Two weeks later, our father left, and five months after that, Social Services removed all four of us from our home. I persuaded the judge to let me go back after Mom completed ninety days of inpatient care, but they said the other kids were too young to return. When she got worse again, they tried to take me back, but we managed to avoid them. We moved a lot, made up new names and stories for ourselves. After a while, Social Services quit trying to find us, but we still mostly hid. Just to be safe."

Dean had trouble swallowing. His throat was tight, and his words squeezed out in a croak. "Inpatient care. You mean rehab?" Drugs, alcohol—which one had been Mom's medication of choice? And how could she have done either when she had children to take care of? What kind of self-centered woman was she?

"No. Psychiatric care. She had severe bipolar disorder. My father couldn't deal with it. When she got really bad, he left. Having a wife who was crazy wasn't good for his business reputation."

Regret that he'd automatically assumed the worst of her mother flashed through Dean. No one wanted to have psychiatric problems, especially with four kids to care for and a husband who'd run out on her.

Obviously her father was the self-centered one. If he couldn't handle his wife's problems, how in hell had he expected the kids to? Why hadn't he taken them with him? How heartless could the bastard be?

"We lost pretty much everything after he left—the house, the car, regular meals. Mom had never worked except to put him through college. Even if she could have held a job, all she knew was waiting tables and being a mom. The court ordered our father to pay child support, but he moved out of state and no one seemed very interested in tracking him down."

When he'd asked about her father earlier, all she'd said was he ran out and never came back. Truth, on the surface, but hiding a lot of ugliness. Dean hated deadbeat fathers. Starting with his secretary's ex, he'd tracked down a bunch of them, always for free to the mothers. Kids suffered enough when marriages ended. If he could help it, they wouldn't be burdened by a lack of funds. By losing *regular meals.* Damn!

Miri went on in the plain, level voice that chilled him as much as her words, relating a nightmare life in the same way he might say, *I had a great childhood.* "We went from a beautiful big house to a one-bedroom apartment with cock-roaches as big as Chloe. Mom did the best she could, but there were times when she couldn't even get out of bed. Other times, she'd go days without sleeping, so manic that she scared us all."

"So you took care of the other kids and your mother." The idea made him hurt. She'd been so young, abandoned unwillingly by her mother, spitefully by her father. A lot of adults couldn't have coped with that situation. How was a child supposed to?

By becoming secretive. Distrusting. Disillusioned. Keep-ing people at arm's length and building a wall around her-self so no one could hurt her again.

"Not well enough. After a while, the state terminated Mom's parental rights and they let Sophy, Oliver and Chloe be adopted."

"Aw, Miri." He hesitated, then shoved back the covers and crossed the few feet between the beds to sit beside her. She didn't flinch or edge away, not even when he laid his hand lightly on hers. "You were ten years old. Your parents couldn't hold the family together. How could you expect to?"

"I was the oldest. It was my responsibility."

"The only responsibilities ten-year-olds are supposed to have are cleaning their rooms, doing their homework and taking out the trash. You weren't responsible. You couldn't be. You give your mother credit for doing her best. You have to give yourself the same credit."

Her soft sigh didn't sound convinced as she rested her chin on her knees. "My name was Ali then. The last time I saw Oliver and Chloe, they were screaming *Ali, Ali!* as the social workers dragged them away. Sophy tried to comfort them, but she was crying, too. She was only six."

Wasn't that a pleasant memory to have burned into a ten-year-old mind? Dean thought, bitter on her behalf. He'd always known she was strong, but he hadn't had a clue exactly how strong, to have survived a childhood like that.

When she remained silent, he gently prompted, "So they were adopted, and you grew up really fast to take care of your mom. Have you seen them since?"

She shook her head.

"Do you know where they are?"

"Oliver's still in North Carolina. Chloe's in Alabama. Sophy…" Her mouth moved, trembling, as she tried to form a smile. "She's in Georgia."

Of course she was. "That's where you're going. To see her."

Another sorry effort at a smile. "Yes. Maybe. Unless she doesn't want…"

To see me. He dragged his fingers through his hair. She blamed herself for not being able to keep the family together—as if she'd had a snowball's chance in hell—and now she was afraid that her sister blamed her, too.

And, hell, who knew? Maybe she did. Maybe Sophy had been too young and too traumatized to remember anything except that in a few short months, she'd lost her entire family and big sister Ali hadn't protected her. Maybe she'd been so traumatized she didn't even remember her big sister at all.

Either of which would break Miri's heart.

Scooting, he bumped her shoulder, nudging her aside, then mimicked her position beside her, only instead of resting his arms on his knees, he slid his left arm around her. "You'll never know what she wants until you try. You could be the best Christmas gift she's ever gotten." He paused, swallowing over the lump in his throat, then hoarsely added, "You've been a pretty damn good one for me."

"Or the worst she's ever had." She paused, too, and he thought she was going to ignore his last statement until she showed the first real emotion since she'd started the conversation. Curiosity. "Even though I'm not giving back the money?"

The idea made him a little squeamish. A criminal shouldn't profit from her crime. Even though the court hadn't ordered restitution, even though as far as the State of Texas was concerned, she'd served her time and had no further obligations, it was just plain wrong to keep money she'd embezzled. Morally, ethically wrong. Just not legally so.

"I can't pretend I don't care about that."

"I earned that money."

"How? By serving fourteen months in jail?"

She tilted her head to gaze up at him. This close he could make out her features. Brown eyes. Cute nose. Lips curved up the slightest bit. "I earned it—at least, part of it—by taking care of my sisters and brother for five months. By taking care of my mother for eight years. By watching my mother die and burying her all by myself. By losing my family and my childhood. By having my entire world ripped apart by the man who'd sworn to love my mother in sickness and in health, when what he really meant was *until* sickness, then he was getting the hell out."

Dean slowly released her to move where he could see her face-to-face. After staring a moment in darkness, he switched on the wall sconce between the beds. Its light was so dim that it took only seconds for his vision to adjust, and then he continued to stare at her.

Slowly he forced his mouth to move. "Mr. Smith is your father."

She extended her hand. "Alicia Miriam Smith. When

Mom died and I switched to Miri, I also took her maiden name, Duncan."

His stare dropped to her hand, small, delicate, but he couldn't move to take it. All he could think in that moment, and the next few, were two words. *That bastard.*

John W. Smith, multimillionaire politician whose strong Christian beliefs and even stronger family values were expected to take him far. The man always accompanied in public by his beautiful wife and their beautiful children, upon whom he lavished time, love and tons of money. The man who'd kept Dean's business running when he'd had tough times. He'd always had so much respect for Mr. Smith.

So much for his character assessment skills.

"Does he know?"

She shook her head. "I thought I would tell him once I'd given Sophy, Oliver and Chloe their shares. Then I thought maybe not. He didn't care about us. I don't care about him."

Shares. The amount of money had been odd: $1,092,673.72. Why not an even $1.1 mil? "You totaled the child support he never paid, didn't you?"

"Plus interest. Each of us gets a share depending on how many years he didn't pay."

It was a lot of money, but Miriam had described their house as big and beautiful and said he'd worried about his sick wife tarnishing his reputation. Likely, the child support had been commensurate with his salary.

"So you'll get the least amount. After getting the money in the first place. That doesn't seem fair."

She managed a real smile. "Most things in life aren't fair. But he owed this money. Taking it was fair. Giving it to my sisters and brother is fair."

It was a lot to take in, and it was a confidence that humbled him, that she could trust him with all the painful aspects of her life. But he still had one question, still needed one answer. "Why are you telling me this now?"

For a long time, she sat silent, then slowly she reached out to touch his hand—not to grip it, just to lay the tips of her fingers on it. "Someone once told me that if what you've been doing isn't working for you, then it's time to change. I—I need a change, Dean."

Chapter 6

Her chest was too tight to manage adequate breath as she waited for him to say something, for a hint that he understood what she was saying. It came when he gently turned his hand over and folded his fingers around hers. "Miriam," he whispered, and the intensity of emotion in his voice brought tears to her eyes.

He leaned forward, still holding her hand in his, and kissed her, the sweetest kiss she'd ever gotten. When it was over, he rested his forehead against hers and raggedly said, "Don't do this tonight, then leave me tomorrow. I've never had my heart broken before, but I'm sure it's not a pretty sight."

"Mine's been broken six times. I can tell you, it's not."

She could practically see him counting silently: her father, her mother, Sophy, Oliver and Chloe. He grinned. "You did like me."

"I did."

"I liked you, too. I still do. More than any other woman I've ever known."

A spasm of uncertainty clamped around her heart. She was so used to not believing, not trusting, that the doubt came automatically, but she forced it away. That was the old Miri, the old life. New Miri had faith in herself and others. New Miri trusted the people she loved and, no matter how she'd denied it, she did love Dean.

He kissed her again, and the uncertainty vanished, replaced by warm, hungry desire. He wanted her. After eight years of being needed too much, then twelve years where no one needed her at all, it was wonderful to be *wanted*.

They made love, fitting together so naturally, desperately and tenderly and lazily, and it was more perfect than she'd ever dared dream of. Just before falling asleep, Dean nuzzled her neck. "Santa never disappoints those who truly believe, Miriam. Welcome to the believers."

A believer. That might have been the nicest compliment anyone had given her.

She dozed fitfully through the rest of the night, waking up too often from dreams about her family. The kids screaming and fighting the social workers. Sophy crying. The last words her sister had said, *What about Boo?*

Every waking moment, it seemed her heart beat faster, her stomach turned queasier. How could she face Sophy again? How could she risk knowing her little sister's life was too full for an unhappy reminder like Miri? She could put Boo in a box, along with the storybook and the motel phone number, address him and drop him at a shipping place. Everyone was doing overnight deliveries this close to Christmas. Sophy would have him on Christmas Eve, and if Miri didn't hear from her in the next few days, she would have her answer.

But when she made the suggestion to Dean while they

ate breakfast, he scowled. "Sure, if you want to take the coward's way out."

"I'm not a coward," she denied even as her internal voice admitted she was. "I'm trusting you, aren't I?"

The scowl transformed into a look of awe that quickly gave way to his usual overconfident grin. "Yeah. You are. But it's still the cowardly way. When did you start looking for Sophy and the others?"

"The day after I buried my mother."

"Twelve years. You planned twelve years for the day you could see Sophy again—you went to *jail* for that—and now you want to back out? You want to send a *note* telling her where the money is?"

Her gaze flickered out the restaurant window to the Charger, where Boo lay covered again in the backseat.

"You've earned this day, Miriam. And you're not going alone." He gripped her hand, resting on the tabletop. "I'll be right there beside you. I'll always be with you."

The words sent a rush of warmth through her. She knew not all promises could be kept. Her father hadn't wanted to keep his; her mother hadn't been able to keep hers. But as long as Dean meant the words, as long as he tried, she would be all right.

"Okay?" he asked when she didn't say anything.

She nodded.

He asked the passing waitress for the check, then said, "So where are we going?"

Her stomach knotted, but she answered anyway. "Copper Lake. East on I-20 until we see the sign."

Within five minutes, they were on their way. She sat stiffly in her seat, holding Boo as tightly as she'd always wished she could have held Sophy, Oliver and Chloe. She stared out the window, anxious and apprehensive, trying to be positive but too used to taking the negative view.

Whichever way it went, she would be okay. Better to know than to forever wonder, right? And whatever happened, at least she would see Sophy. She would be able to put an adult face to the sweet, brown-eyed, pigtailed, blonde kid who'd followed her everywhere.

It seemed as if the trip from Dallas to Atlanta had taken weeks, but the miles to the Copper Lake exit flew past. Long before Miri was ready, a sign announced the town limits, then businesses began appearing on either side of the road.

"Where do we find her?" Dean asked quietly.

"She has a shop downtown on Oglethorpe. It's called Hanging by a Thread." Her voice was breathy, and as he turned onto the street running along the south side of the square, she could hardly manage to fill her lungs. Copper Lake was a small town; downtown couldn't be more than a few square blocks. She was so close to Sophy that she might be able to scream her name and be heard.

Oglethorpe was the next street. Dean paused at the intersection, looked left, then right and said, "There it is." He turned right and found a parking space a few yards down.

Hanging by a Thread was a quilt shop and occupied the bottom floor of an old Victorian house, with Sophy's apartment on the second floor. It was a lovely, homey place, with a picket fence, rockers on one side of the porch and a swing on the other, along with tasteful Christmas decorations. Matching fresh-cut wreaths hung on each of the double doors, tied with elaborate red bows. It was perfect for a girl who'd lost her real home when she was six.

Please, God, let her be happy. Let Oliver and Chloe have good lives, too.

A few clicks and grumbles from the settling engine were the only sound inside the car until Dean took her hand. "Are you ready?"

"No. There's a coffee shop over there." She gestured back

to the square, even though the thought of hot brew made her stomach flip-flop. "We could get some coffee, maybe something to eat."

"We finished breakfast less than two hours ago."

"Maybe we should just walk around a little. See what else is here. Or find a motel. Or—"

His kiss silenced her. It was fierce and passionate and turned her brain inside out. While she tried to recover, he got out, circled the car and opened the door, taking her hand, pulling her from the vehicle. "You can do this. *We* can do it."

She tugged free before he could close the door and grabbed her backpack. After emptying her clothes onto the seat, she stuffed Boo inside, slung it over her shoulder, then sighed deeply. *Exhale terror. Inhale confidence.* What she actually inhaled was the fragrance of Dean's cologne, a reminder of the man himself, and that was close enough to confidence for her.

The gate in the picket fence was propped open, and the steps creaked as they climbed them. The scent of pine tickled her nose as she reached for the knob. It was only the pressure of Dean's hand in the small of her back that allowed her to open the door and step inside.

Fabric took up most of the space, in every color, every pattern. Finished quilts hung on the walls and on racks, while unfinished ones were draped across tables. Christmas classics performed in blues style played softly in the background, and the lone person in the store, her back to the door, sang along while she worked at a large table. Her silky blond hair was fixed in an intricate French braid and tied with a red-and-green velvet bow, and she wore a white shirt with neatly pressed pants and flats.

Sophy. Miri's knees went weak, and she would have turned and fled if Dean hadn't anticipated the move and stopped her with his arm around her middle.

Though there had been no ding of a bell when they'd opened the door, the rush of fresh air or maybe the change of pressure had alerted Sophy to someone's presence. "I'll be right with you," she said without looking up. "Just give me a minute to finish pinning this section."

Dean pushed Miri along the aisle toward the work area in the center of the shop. She wanted to stop, to flee, to race to her sister, throw her arms around her and cry, but she was too stunned to do anything but follow his direction, stopping finally when a cutting table blocked her route.

"Okay, that should hold it." Sophy turned, revealing clear brown eyes, perfect nose, delicately shaped mouth. She was beautiful, with the same sweet, happy smile Miri remembered best in her dreams.

She couldn't speak, didn't know what to say, how to start, whether she could say anything at all. Sophy looked curiously from her to Dean, then back again. Slowly her eyes widened, and the fabric squares she held fell soundlessly to the floor. "Ali? Oh, my God, *Ali?*"

Miri took a step and bumped the table, surprised it was there. With a quiet, "It's okay," Dean nudged her around it, and by the time she cleared the other side, Sophy was there, grabbing her in a breath-stealing embrace.

Something inside Miri broke, some ice, some force that had kept her going the past twenty years, and she sagged against her younger sister, tears seeping from her eyes. For the first time since she'd sat at her mother's deathbed, she cried.

"I've wondered, I've hoped, I've prayed… Oh, Ali, I thought I'd never see you again!" Sophy pushed her back a little, her hands tightly gripping Miri's, and gave her a sweeping look. "You haven't changed except for getting taller. We still look so much alike except you're still so gorgeous."

They did look alike, though Sophy's features had such sweet softness to them. Miri knew she looked harder, tougher, but that was okay. Toughness could fade.

Finally Miri found her voice, and of course, her comment was inane. "You're all grown-up."

"Twenty years will do that. How did you find me?"

"The internet. You and Oliver and Chloe." *And dear old Dad.* "Have you seen…?"

Tears welling, Sophy shook her head. "I tried a few times to find them, to find you, but…" Her eyes darkened with sadness. "I did find Mom's obituary a few years ago. I went to Asheville, to see if you were still there, or the little ones, and I visited her grave. Have you seen the kids?"

"Not yet. I wanted to see you first. I wanted to bring you—" Miri freed her hands and tugged the backpack from her shoulder. First she pulled out the storybook, rewarded with instant recognition, then she removed the bear.

Sophy's eyes lit with delight. "Boo! Oh, my gosh, I can't believe you kept him for me. Mom and Dad—I mean, my adoptive parents—bought me every teddy bear they could find to replace him. They couldn't accept that he was irreplaceable." She hugged him, then swiped at her eyes. "Oh, Ali, thank you!"

Dean came to stand beside Miri, and she glanced at him long enough to see that she was definitely going to hear *I told you so* from him a time or three. "Sophy, this is Dean Montgomery. He's, um…" *My boyfriend? My lover? The man I love most in the world?*

He offered his hand, and her sister took it. "I haven't asked yet, but I plan to be your brother-in-law soon."

Sophy kissed his cheek. "Welcome to the family, Dean."

"Yeah, welcome to the family, Dean."

The voice came from behind them, rough, mocking, sending chills through Miri. She'd heard only a few words from that voice, but she recognized it. Stiffly, she turned to face him and his buddy.

The men from the bus station.

Muscles taut, Dean moved to block both Miri and Sophy from the men's view. He recognized the flaring of satisfaction that he was right; the run-in with them hadn't been coincidence. Given that they were both holding guns, he would have much preferred to be wrong. The fact that his own weapon was nestled in the small of his back didn't offer much comfort, not with the two women behind him at risk.

"What do you want?" he asked, feeling Miri's trembling even though she wasn't actually touching him.

"Same thing we wanted in Dallas. Her." That was the man who'd stepped out of the shadows and clipped him on the jaw. He was average height, muscle-bound and ugly as a monkey. The other guy was still grinning, just like that night. "We'd've been happy to settle for just her then, but Mr. Garvin said if she led us to anyone else, especially a pretty little blonde who looks just like her, we could take you all."

"You'd really risk life in prison for a cut of $110,000?" Dean shook his head. "You're stupider than you look."

The smiling guy snorted. "There's no risk if you don't get caught. Besides, we're getting a hell of a lot more than that."

Monkey Guy moved a few slow steps closer. "Let's talk stupid, Montgomery. First, remember the other night when you told us you were carrying a .45? Give it up. Set it on that table in front of you."

Grimly Dean pulled the pistol from its holster and, holding it by two fingers, carefully set it on the table.

The man shoved the gun into his coat pocket. "Second, you really believe Smith hired you to recover his money, don't you? With all his millions, he don't give a damn about what she took. He knew you'd had a thing with her. He knew you was the one she's most likely to trust. As long as we kept her scared enough to stay with you, we could follow right where she went." He paused. "And then clean up."

"You put a GPS tracker on my car before she was released." Disgust with himself tasted ugly. He'd helped them keep track of her. He'd led them here, damn it. Some P.I. he was.

Then a worse realization settled in his gut. "Smith knows who she really is."

A soft gasp came from behind him. Miri had thought Smith was clueless about her, that he'd written her off as part of a disastrous practice family, but she'd been wrong. He hadn't forgotten, and he had far more than money to lose. God, how could he have misjudged the bastard so completely?

Monkey Guy nodded. "He seen some pictures of her after she was locked up. Didn't take him long to figure it out."

Of course not. Sophy had been six years old the last time she'd seen Miri, but she'd needed only moments to recognize her.

"A man in his position, he's gotta do what he's gotta do."

Twenty-four hours ago, Dean had believed the man's hype. Now he knew Smith was a snake just like these guys. He would do anything to maintain the false image he'd created. Even order his own daughter killed. And if his second daughter and Dean had to die, too, he could live with that, as long as his precious reputation remained intact.

Monkey Guy shifted his attention to Sophy. "You got a back room to this place?"

"Y-y-yes." She raised one trembling hand and pointed to a door half hidden by a hanging quilt.

"Go on. You two ladies first."

Still clutching the bear, Sophy led the way. After a few steps, Miri caught up with her, wrapping her arm around her, murmuring, "I'm so sorry. I never would have come here if I'd known…" And Sophy whispering back, "It's okay, Ali, it's okay."

The storeroom had originally been the old house's kitchen. The cupboards remained, but the appliances had been removed, with large cubbies built in their spaces. It offered no weapon, no cover for the women, no island to hide behind, no back door to escape through. Whatever Dean did, he would have to take out both men quickly to minimize danger to Miri and Sophy.

Once they were all in the room, the three of them against the counter where the sink would have been, the two men just inside the door, Smiley asked, "You got any rope around here?"

Sophy's head trembled left to right. Miri scoffed. "It's a quilt shop, moron. She's got needles and thread and patterns and fabric."

And really sharp scissors, though none were lying around at the moment.

Monkey Guy nodded, and Smiley began searching cabinets. The best he could come up with was a spool of wide grass-green ribbon dotted with striped Easter eggs. He started with Sophy, pulling her away from the counter, tying her hands behind her back, shoving her to the floor six feet away.

Miri eased a step closer to Dean, looking up at him, her expression fearful. "I'm sorry."

"Me, too."

"I love you."

Typical Miri. Admitting something that important when it just might be too late to mean anything. He was about to murmur the words back when a faint sickly smile touched her lips and she mouthed, *Get ready.*

Get *ready?* What the hell was she planning?

The answer came quickly enough when Smiley reached for her. As he tried to turn her, she danced away to the side, forcing him to move with her in a struggle to gain control. "Please, don't tie my hands, please. I spent too much time in handcuffs, I really can't handle it, please, please—"

Her last words were drowned by a scream. Not smiling anymore, Smiley spun away in a crouch, cursing, hands over his face and blood streaming over his fingers. The knife she'd lifted from the glove box, its blade bloodied, was in her right hand, the sight almost enough to turn Dean's stomach before he launched himself at Monkey Guy.

They both hit the floor hard, and the man's gun flew from his hand, striking the floor in the shop, discharging once with a thunderous *bang* before sliding to a stop. Straddling him, Dean fumbled in the guy's jacket for his own gun, bringing the barrel a scant inch from the sweet spot right between the man's eyes. "I warned you," he said softly. "This HK will make your Christmas *very* unmerry. Don't even blink."

Without taking his gaze from Monkey Guy, he asked, "Miri, you all right?"

"I am. I've got his gun."

He grinned. "I warned you about Blondie, too. You don't want the kind of trouble that she'll bring." He risked a glance at her then, bloody knife in one hand, Smiley's pistol in the other, looking as if she could continue kicking ass all day, and added with certainty, "But I do."

Christmas Eve was sunny but cold, the snow they'd left behind scheduled to arrive before midnight. Miri hoped it would. A white Christmas would be nice, wouldn't it? It was cozy here in Sophy's apartment. More important, she wasn't alone. Her sister was there, she still loved Miri and she wanted to share their lives. Her first Christmas miracle ever.

No, the second. Dean was the first.

She and Sophy had talked until their voices were hoarse. Miri had told her…almost everything. Not the details of the first eight years. If Sophy believed the time when it was just Miri and their mom had been much better than reality, what could it hurt? Dean knew the truth, and that was enough for her.

It was late afternoon. The shop was closed. The two men who'd threatened them the day before were in the Copper Lake jail, one bearing stitches thanks to Miri's knife work, and all they'd gotten for Christmas were charges of kidnapping and attempted murder. They'd talked until they were hoarse, too, about their boss and his boss, John W. Smith, and the conspiracy to preserve the great man's reputation.

Now she and Sophy sat at opposite ends of the sofa in her living room, a fire blazing, their third round of hot cocoa gone, quiet for the first time in hours. Dean had gone out, but he would be back soon to spend Christmas Eve with Sophy's parents. Her mother had come over that morning, greeting them like long-lost family.

Family. That was all Miri had wanted for Christmas. She was the luckiest person in the world.

Heavy treads sounded on the steps outside, then Dean let himself in. His hair was windblown, his cheeks red and snowflakes dusted his shoulders. He hung his coat on a rack near the door, took a small package from the pocket, then came to kiss the top of her forehead before taking a seat across from them. "Got to open a present before we go to the Marchands' house," he said, setting the box in the middle of the coffee table.

"Oh, good." Sophy jumped to her feet, disappeared into her bedroom, then returned with a very large box, placing it on the floor near Miri. "Open Dean's first. It'll make mine even more appropriate."

Miri's hand shook as she picked up Dean's box. It was beautifully wrapped with a shiny gold bow, too small to be anything besides a jeweler's box. It could be earrings or maybe a pendant, but deep in her heart she knew it was a ring. *I plan to be your brother-in-law soon,* he'd told Sophy.

Miri planned to let him.

She removed the paper carefully—the first time she'd gotten a gift in years—to reveal the deep blue case and opened the lid. The ring inside was beautiful, a pearl set in gold, a diamond on each side. Blinking away tears, she looked up to find Dean watching her intensely.

"You saved my life. Now it's yours."

"You saved mine right back." She slid the ring on her fourth finger. "It's perfect."

He came to kiss her, a long, sweet promise, then nudged her so he could sit beside her. "I love you," he murmured as Sophy moved the big box to the table.

She smiled tremulously at him before her sister said, "Now it's my turn."

This gift wasn't wrapped. It was just a large box, the flaps folded to secure the top. Her name was written in marker across one flap, along with a date five years earlier. Inside was a large tissue-wrapped bundle. Laying it on the table, she began unrolling it, finally revealing a large section of an intricate quilt.

"It's a Double Wedding Ring," Sophy said. "I made one for each of us."

Five years ago. Even then, her sister had been thinking about her. Even knowing she might never see her again, she'd created this for her. Miri wiped tears from her eyes. "Thank you. It's beautiful. I should hang it like a museum piece."

Sophy swiped her own eyes. "Oh, hell, no, Ali. I expect you two to conceive my nieces and nephews under it."

Miri hugged the quilt. She would never be apart from her sister again, no matter how many miles separated them. The hours of work and skill Sophy had put into the quilt ensured that.

Clearing her throat, Sophy stood. "I guess we should get going—"

"Wait." At Miri's interruption, she sat down again, but Miri stood. Boo was in a place of honor under the Christmas tree, and she'd seen a pair of scissors in a drawer in the kitchen. She got both, then sat on the coffee table. "Don't worry," she said when she saw the concern in her sister's eyes, then she carefully snipped a dozen stitches from the bear's side. Once the hole was big enough, she began withdrawing flat packets of money, stacking them neatly, until Boo looked anorexic instead of well-loved and robust.

"Remember all the child support our father never paid?" She pushed the money toward Sophy. "Merry Christmas, Soph."

"Oh, my God. Ali, I can't take— You should keep— This is—" After a moment she looked up. "Wow."

After they restuffed the bear, securing his side with safety pins, Sophy gathered gifts from under the tree while Dean helped Miri into her coat. She pulled the pink hat over her hair, then looked up at him. "Do you still care that I'm not giving back the money?"

"After your father hired someone to kill you? No way."

"I'm sorry I don't have a gift for you."

"You *are* my gift, Miriam." His grin, quick and smug and more charming than ever, warmed her. "And I plan to keep unwrapping you for a long, long time."

* * * * *

In memory of my mother, Wanda Strain,
and my nephew, Kevin Dillman,
who loved the holidays. I know you're enjoying
Christmas in heaven.

LINDA CONRAD

A Chance Reunion

To my dear mother,
who always made Christmas special,
even if that meant having spaghetti
every Christmas Eve. I can make the spaghetti,
Mom, but it's never the same without you.

Chapter 1

That danged statue of a reindeer sitting on the bar nearby grinned at nothing in particular and blinked its red nose in perpetual holiday cheer.

Gage Chance didn't know whether to ignore the too-cute decoration or pull his weapon and blast the miserable cheery monstrosity right off its perch. *Christmas*. To quote a smarter man than he would ever be, "Humbug."

Downing the last of his longneck, Gage dropped a few bills on the bar and slid off the stool. Tired and frustrated, he was done—for the night and with this trip.

The trip had been a long shot, anyway. As a professional investigator, he knew better than to take anonymous tips he couldn't verify. Yet when the email showed up in his inbox, he'd wanted so bad to believe.

The person you seek can be found in the Piñon Lake area of California.

That "person you seek" line had to be referring to his lost little sister. He and his brothers had tried in vain for twenty-one years to get a line on Cami's whereabouts. Even to this day, the FBI still carried an open case file on her.

She'd been kidnapped from their ranch in Texas at the age of four by their mother's sister and apparently sold to the highest bidder in Los Angeles. But that's where the trail ran cold. The aunt's body was discovered in the L.A. morgue a few years later, dead of an overdose. His family had been concentrating their search for Cami in the southern California area ever since.

Raking a hand through his hair and resettling his Stetson, he walked toward the door and the too-festive twinkle lights beyond on the street. Even though he'd tried for twenty-four hours after that message came in to find an original IP address for the sender, the internet trail petered out in a maze of international switchbacks and phony addresses. He should've guessed it was a gag. Or worse, that it could've been someone who wanted to get him out of Chance for a few days.

Stepping out the door into the lightly falling snow, he pulled his satellite phone from his jacket's pocket. Better call one of his brothers back at the ranch and make sure everything was okay.

Travis answered at the main house. "It's a little late, bro. Remember the time difference? We have a kid in the house and just got her back in bed." Travis's yawn came through loud and clear.

Gage figured it was more a case of his older brother's new bride waiting for him in bed. But he wasn't in the mood at the moment to rib Travis about his nonsleeping, newly-wed habits.

Travis came to the point first. "Have you found anything that leads to Cami?"

"Sorry about the hour," Gage mumbled. It was only eight-thirty in Piñon Lake and holiday tourists were still shopping along the quaint village streets, making it seem much earlier. "I've found zip here. Two days of walking around the town and resorts and showing Cami's age-enhanced photo to everyone I meet has brought me exactly nothing. No one recognizes her. I've had it. I'm planning on flying back to the Bar-C tomorrow."

"Good. Not that we need that plane you're flying anytime soon, but it's only a week to Christmas and the family wants you back on the ranch to join in the celebrations."

Gage was never in the mood for Christmas. Even talking about it depressed him. But he didn't say anything to upset his brother. Instead, he checked with Travis to be sure his P.I. office in the little town of Chance was secure and then bid his brother good-night.

As he pocketed the phone, laughter rang out like tinkling bells on the sidewalk up ahead. Couples and small groups of young people tromped down the town's streets past evergreen and ivy that shimmered with thousands of tiny white lights. They seemed to be doing last-minute Christmas shopping and trying to stay warm by stopping at every bar on the strip. It was only a three-block walk back to his hotel, but Gage would rather take a taxi than have to face this much gaiety.

Still, taxis were nonexistent at the moment and few cars could be seen on the streets. Some shops were already closed for the night and others would shut down soon. With this much drinking going on, he imagined everyone walking the sidewalks now must be staying over in the town's hotel like he was. Or maybe they were already registered at the ski resorts located out near the slopes and planned on taking a shuttle bus back later tonight. Probably a lot more partying would be going on at the resorts. Something he could definitely do without.

Setting his chin and tugging the brim of his hat lower on his forehead, he started out down the street. As he passed along in front of the few still-open retail stores, he glanced in the windows, trying to decide whether he had the energy or the wherewithal to stop in each one and ask after his sister.

He didn't. This much Christmas cheer was getting him down.

When was the last time he'd actually celebrated Christmas? Had to be at least six years ago. He knew that because five years ago he'd lost all interest in Christmas—and in just about everything else, for that matter.

Up ahead of him by a few yards, a young man and woman stood arm in arm, gazing into a bridal shop window with rapture on their faces. Gage's stomach turned. Didn't they know that life was far too fragile to pin their hopes on love and romance? They shouldn't let the holiday season overtake their better judgment. If they had to get married, better that they do it in the dead heat of summer when their thinking would be clearer. When ice and snow and good cheer could not mess with their hearts and forever leave them adrift in the cold.

He'd succumbed to the fantasy of love and marriage one snowy Christmas himself. And before the next Christmas rolled around, he was single again and doubled over in the worst kind of grief imaginable.

Sticking his hands in his coat pockets, Gage drew in a frosty breath and walked around the starry-eyed couple. Okay, so his two older brothers had managed their spring and summer weddings during the past year. And so far so good for them. He wished them both long and happily married lives.

Forcing back some of the gloom that had been his constant companion, he reminded himself that his family would be celebrating Christmas even if he wasn't in the mood. The love of his brothers was all that had gotten him through the worst of times. The bumpy road that had been the past five years. All the grief and despair. What would've become of him without his family?

They deserved to have their cheerful holiday, uninterrupted by his depression. Searching for their baby sister was one way he was trying to pay them back. But what could he do to make this holiday better for them?

Presents. He hadn't given family gifts a single thought. Not in years.

Sucking in enough air to clear his head, he decided this year had to be different. This year he would make the best of it. Bring presents. Eat and drink too much. And maybe even act as Santa Claus for the youngsters in the family.

Celebrating Christmas could be the trick that finally pushed him over the hump. And afterward, maybe he would begin to live again.

Glancing into the next window, he was surprised to see a jewelry shop full of exquisite handmade pieces. Just the thing to please his sisters-in-law and the little girls in the family.

As he stood in the chill night air, smiling at all the beautifully crafted rings, necklaces and earrings, he caught sight of an interesting brooch on display in the back. It looked familiar. In fact, he would swear that...

Tilting his head and pressing his nose close to the glass, he studied the multicolored stone pattern of the piece. Son of a gun. It couldn't be.

But danged if it wasn't. The more he looked at it the more convinced he was that the design was identical to the traditional brand used on Bar-C cattle. That same pattern appeared everywhere in Chance, Texas. On the ranch's gates. On stationery. On buildings. He couldn't be mistaken. He'd been seeing it for the whole of his lifetime.

How was it possible for it to appear here?

A feminine hand slipped into the window display as some clerk from inside moved the brooch forward so he could get a better look. But that hand only made his emotions churn higher.

Something hard and shocking punched him deep in the chest with no warning. Just look at that slender hand. Those short but clean fingernails polished to a clear, high sheen. The long fingers that might be better suited for piano playing than anything else. He would know that hand anywhere. It, and the body attached to it, had appeared in his dreams often enough.

But that's all that hand had been for the past five years, just a dream. Not reality. Not like this. Glancing up, his gaze locked with that of a young woman. She'd been smiling as she moved the jewelry around for him to see. But the smile froze on her lips and the blood drained from her face as she stood motionless staring into his eyes.

What the hell?

It was her. But not her.

His Alicia had soft hazel eyes. This stranger's eyes were green. Still, he immediately thought of his dead wife.

Stunned, Gage lost his cool. Whoever this person might be, she was almost the spitting image of Alicia. But not quite. Gasping for a ragged breath, he started toward the shop door, determined to talk to her. Was she a relative of Alicia's? For months he'd searched for any family after his wife's death.

She'd always said she was alone in the world. Her parents were gone and she didn't know of anyone else. His many brothers and big family had intrigued her. She'd cherished finally having a family around to count on.

This stranger seemed like proof that there had been other relatives.

After swinging open the glass door and barging into the shop, his gaze took in the small retail space. No one was around. In the next second an old man with a shock of pure white hair came from somewhere in the back of the place. He stepped beside one of the glass cases and narrowed his gaze at Gage.

"May I help you, Mr. Cowboy?" the man asked with a heavy Irish lilt. "Something for your wife, I'd be guessing?"

Gage threw a glance at his left hand where the gold band still adorned his ring finger. "Not married. I'm a widower. Besides, I don't need that kind of help. I want the woman that was just here. Where is she? Where'd she go?"

"Excuse me?" The man's cherubic expression became more pronounced. "My English is rusty, then. What is it you require?" He looked like a sweet-faced Irish angel.

Gage took three quick steps and faced the man squarely. "Don't give me that." He wanted to put his hands around the guy's neck and choke the information out of him. "The woman was here. I saw her in the window. Where is she?"

"Sorry…"

The old man barely had the word out when Gage brushed past him and went through a doorway into the back of the store. A cold draft told him there had to be a back way out, but it was too dark to see much. After fumbling around for a moment, he found the door and shoved it open.

Stepping out into an empty alleyway, he checked to his right and left. Nothing. Not one single soul could be seen all the way to the end of the block.

Lost her.

Snow was falling in thick sheets by now. He glanced

down and spotted a woman's shoe print a few feet along the pavement. But the print was quickly covered over in the mass of white powder being dumped from the sky.

Damn it.

Gritting his teeth, he stormed back into the store and confronted the old man again. "I want the truth. None of your crap about not understanding me. Who was she and where do I find her?"

"There was no she. 'Tis only me."

Furious, it was all he could do not to shake the old man. "I want to talk to your boss. The manager. Or the owner of the store."

"I am the proprietor of this establishment. I sell by way of the finest in handcrafted jewelry. Beads and semiprecious stones. Brendan Keane, at your service, boyo."

Oh, man, this conversation was proving impossible. The old guy was a charming snake oil salesman.

"So you are not going to tell me who she was. The one I clearly saw with long, slender fingers and bewitching green eyes." Not a question. Gage knew he would get nothing.

"I canna tell what is not in my power to tell."

Fine. He didn't suppose he would get a straight answer about the design on the brooch, either. But he tried.

"Would you like to buy the piece?" the old guy asked when Gage inquired who made it. "It's a one of a kind."

That wasn't an answer to the question, but he knew getting decent answers was hopeless.

"Never mind," he told Brendan Keane as he turned his back and headed out the front door.

Feeling raw and on the verge of desperation, Gage checked the nearby stores. Maybe someone would know the woman. But the stores all seemed closed up tight. Everything had gone dark while he'd been in the jewelry store. Carefully he strode down the slippery sidewalk in the other direction, determined to make it back to his hotel room in record time. He had the whole night to track her down on the internet.

And by God, that was just what he intended to do. For years, he'd honed the craft of finding people until he was the best in the business. If anyone could uncover the woman whose hands and eyes belonged to Alicia, it was him.

It was him. Of all the people in the world that she'd hoped never to see again, Gage Chance was number one on the list.

As Elana Kelly ran through the back streets, her heart pounded erratically—for more reasons than just the quickened pace. How had he found her? For five years she'd worked hard at weaving an intricate cloak of invisibility around herself. It seemed impossible that even someone as good at tracking as Gage could have found her.

But if he'd found her, then her father and Andrei could not be far behind. Oh, God. She would have to run again. Tonight. It would be much harder to begin again now than it had been all those years ago. Still, she had no choice.

Keeping to the back streets, she took extra time in the hopes that he would not be able to follow her in the heavy snowfall. He must not track her to the little house where she'd been starting to feel at home.

As she ran, she thought about Gage. And hungered for more time with him. To touch and be touched. To share a moment out of her life with someone who cared. With just that first quick glance into his face, she knew her love for him had not dimmed one iota in the past five years.

She rubbed a fist against her chest and dragged more cold air into her lungs.

In so many ways, he hadn't changed in five years. His hair might be a little longer. And his jawline sported a five-o'clock shadow he'd never been known for in the past. But as she'd swum in his beloved gaze, her heart recognized in that instant the same man she'd fallen madly in love with years before.

The only man she'd ever loved. And the only man she was ever likely to love in this lifetime—or the next.

Not good. So not good.

But his physical presence had always pulled on her in a powerful way. Overwhelming and intense. It was the reason they'd both succumbed so fast to the startling lust, leaving her good sense and fear in the dust of their lovemaking.

For five years she'd blamed herself for giving in to the attraction—for falling hard and fast when her life had not been her own. She had not been free to take a lover, let alone a husband. Now, after a single glimpse into his eyes, she remembered how impossible it had been to resist him. One look and she was cooked.

Out of breath, she reached the back stairs that took her to the second-floor apartment above the small house belonging to the Keanes. Taking them two at a time, she dug her key out of her pocket and let herself in the front door.

"Maeve!" she rasped as she entered the foyer, her tone an octave too high. "It's me. I need help."

"Shush," the familiar voice called out, sight unseen. "Keep your voice down. I just put the darlin' one to bed."

Elana dashed around the corner into the front room. "Good. I hope she sleeps through this."

Maeve Keane looked up from her book, blinking across the rim of her glasses. "What's wrong?"

"I've been found out. He's here."

"Who's here?" A look of pure panic crossed the older woman's face. "Not your father?"

"Thankfully, no. But he won't be too far behind." Elana stood in the center of the room, wringing her hands. "It's my husband. The private investigator. I don't know how this happened. He's good, but so are we."

Maeve set down her book and came to her side. "No sense crying over what's done, dearie. You need to pack, and we need a plan."

Elana drew in a shaky breath. "I want to talk to Brendan first. He was…"

As if on cue, the man himself came through the front door and quickly locked it again.

"The stranger gave up and went off in the other direction," Brendan said as he entered the front room. "I locked up the store, and I'm sure he didn't follow. Who was he?"

"The man I was married to. In Texas." Elana fought the sudden tears. She didn't have time to feel sorry for herself.

"Ah, yes," Brendan said as if that explained it all. "But he wouldn't be a danger to you."

With her hands and knees shaking badly, Elana plopped down in an overstuffed chair. "No. Not him. And I didn't think my father knew about our marriage. Still, you know Andrei's father and my own both have devious ways of finding things out. It was fear for my husband's life that sent me into hiding in the first place. And now…"

"Does he know about the child?" Maeve's eyes were full of sadness.

"No. And he can't." And that knowledge was killing her—slowly but surely. "He's such a decent man. Not like us. He would want to be in his child's life. He would demand a chance to protect her. I can't let him do that."

"He thinks you're dead, Elana." Brendan stood nodding his head and watching for her reaction.

"What? How do you know that?"

"He told me he was a widower."

"Then how…?" Her mind was a jumble. "He found me by coincidence? That's impossible. Isn't it?"

Brendan rubbed at his chin. "Seems like a million to one long shot. But who knows?" He came to stand beside her chair. "Pack and leave tonight. We've taken precautions, but the faster you leave the better."

"But where will I go? And what about Gay?" A gray panic was edging in around the corners of her mind. "I can't drag her out in the middle of the night."

Maeve took her by the hand. "My Brendan will make new arrangements for all of us. Get new papers. It should only take a few days. In the meantime, we'll keep the darlin' with us. Or take her over to the Boswells if we spot danger."

Elana almost couldn't bear the thought of starting all over again. But she knew she must do whatever necessary to keep everyone safe.

"You hide yourself at that cabin up on the ridge—just for a day or two until everything is ready."

"Gay…" How could she leave her daughter behind? It would be much too difficult.

"It will be better to split you two up until we're ready to travel. You have to stay out of sight. The little one would never understand that." Brendan bent to help her to her feet. "Go pack a bag now, dearie. You must be on your way to the cabin before daylight."

Standing on knees that felt like mush, Elana tried to steel herself for the coming days. The temptation to go to Gage and confess, to let him help her and their child, was so strong it nearly bent her in two.

But she couldn't. She'd understood long ago that the biggest danger was to him. So she'd better not. She would stick with the Keanes. Take their protection. And pray that Gage would think he'd been seeing things and let it go.

Let her stay dead.

Chapter 2

Soft footsteps on the frozen alleyway alerted Gage that someone was coming. He crouched lower, losing himself in shadows between the Dumpster and the brick wall at his back.

The snow had stopped falling right after midnight, but temperatures dropped precipitously over the past few hours. Daybreak's lavender light diffused his view of the back door to the jewelry shop. He could see well enough, though. If the person coming down the alley was the half owner of the store, the one he'd been waiting hours to see, she'd be within his view in a few seconds.

Flexing his fingers against the cold, Gage held his breath. A master at waiting under difficult circumstances, surveillance was his middle name.

Investigation was another one of his better talents. It hadn't taken more than a few hours last night to come up with verification that a woman named Elana Kelly owned half interest in the jewelry store. That fact had been noted as part of the tax record. But there didn't seem to be any address listed for her.

He'd also found a recent photo from an article in the local weekly featuring the artists and craftsmen around Piñon Lake. However, her photo was not of her face like those of the other artists. Her picture showed only her hands holding the brooch, the one designed like the Bar-C brand, and a necklace she'd made to go with it. Those hands, still the ones he'd dreamed of, gave her away without him seeing her face. This was the woman he sought.

The article went on to say she'd come to the town of Piñon Lake four years ago with her infant daughter and they'd been welcomed into the artistic community here. The idea of a baby threw him, so he spent the next few hours trying to find records on the birth of a child with that last name anywhere in California during that time frame. And came up with nada. Then he expanded the search to look for any trace of Elana Kelly anywhere in the world before she came here. He found a few by that name but none close in age.

Finding nothing threw big red flags up in his mind. He was good at internet research. Real good. If he couldn't find anything, it was because there was nothing there to find. Whoever this woman was, she had not come into this world as Elana Kelly.

So who was she? Part of a witness protection program? The feds excelled at making up new backgrounds; he knew because his eldest brother had been an agent in the program at one time. But no background info at all seemed odd. Made him wonder if she was running from something— or someone.

At that fleeting thought, the figure of a woman slowly crept down the alley and stopped at the jewelry store's door. Her back was to him as she fumbled to put a key in the lock and let herself in. He didn't get a good look at her face, but she seemed the right size and height.

He waited for her to go inside and close the door before he dashed across the alley to see if she'd locked it. She hadn't. *Not too smart, lady.* Good thing he wasn't a robber or ready to assault her. This was not the time of day to be leaving yourself or your store vulnerable.

Turning the knob, he prayed that the old door's hinges wouldn't squeak in the cold. Unfortunately, the door didn't oblige.

"Stop!" The lights came on and the woman he sought stood three feet away next to a safe.

And she had a gun pointed straight in his direction. "Don't make another move, boyo, or I'll be shooting you with this Taser."

Not a gun, then. Still, he didn't care for the idea of hitting the deck, laid out in the kind of pain he knew those defensive weapons could cause.

"Easy, darlin'." He slowly raised his hands above his head. "I'm not here to hurt you. I just want to talk. You left the door open."

"And it's 5:30 a.m., I'm thinking." The heavy Irish lilt in her voice captured his attention. She narrowed her eyes at him. "Stalking me, are you? I should call the police."

He held his breath and waited, pretty sure the cops were the last thing she'd want. For some reason this woman wanted to hide her real identity.

The next words out of her mouth told him he'd been right. "You said talk? Are you lost, then?"

She lowered the Taser, which wasn't particularly bright. But Gage filled his lungs and grinned, trying to make her feel more at ease. Before he could answer, she hastily stuffed her coat pocket with a wad of bills she must've taken from the safe, then shut the safe door and set her mouth as if waiting for an explanation.

Her eyes flared at him and for the moment, it didn't matter one bit that they were green and not brown.

"Alicia?"

"Who?" Quick flashes of hard steel appeared in those darkened pupils of hers. A harsh expression, it disappeared as quickly as it arrived, unnerving him. Such a look would never have appeared in Alicia's eyes.

"Alicia. My late wife. Sorry. It's just you look enough like her that you could be her twin."

But as he studied the woman now, he saw the differences. Subtle. A few extra pounds, which looked good on this woman but would have swamped his thin-boned wife. A slightly different angle on the tilt of her chin, making her seem somehow stronger than his Alicia. Those things along with the short red hair, the distinct accent and the hard look in her green eyes combined to stop his heart from racing with hope.

Elana wasn't at all sure she could pull this off. She was good at lying. Really good. After all, it was her heritage. And she'd gone to a lot of trouble to put together this disguise, even taking the extra step of having a new chin implant done by a plastic surgeon.

But this was Gage. Her Gage. And her body was already reacting to being this close. Straightening her shoulders, she locked her shaking knees and prepared as if going to battle.

"The name is Elana Kelly." Her voice sounded husky and her accent thick, and she hoped that would embellish her disguise. "You said your late wife's name was Alicia. What is your name, then?"

"Sorry again. Gage Chance. From Chance, Texas. And

before she married me, my wife's name was Alicia Peters. Are you sure you two aren't related?"

"Not that I've ever heard, no." And in fact, Alicia Peters had never been born. That name was just one of several aliases she'd used since starting to run. Actually rather glad to be rid of that name for good, she'd never cared much for it, anyway.

Gage cocked his head and stared at her. She could feel the sexual tension in every inch of her body. Her face automatically warmed and a tiny drop of sweat rolled down the back of her neck. Good thing she'd inherited her father's ancestors' European skin coloring that didn't show a blush.

But come to think of it, Gage had always somehow managed to know when he'd gotten to her, despite the embarrassment not showing on her face.

The damned man gave her another of his sexy grins and the heat increased. Holy Mother of God. She had to get away from him now. Before she fell into his arms and begged him to take her right this instant.

"This may sound a bit rude, but you seemed so—melancholy. May I ask what happened to your wife?" Now, why had she said that? She needed to get away from him, not keep him talking.

"Five years ago she drowned—or at least the police presumed her dead—in an icy river."

"You're not so sure of the facts?" And the minute he'd started talking about it, she knew she was in big trouble.

"I am sure. At least, I was until I saw you." He shook his head as if to clear the memories. "I searched, swam and dove under the bridge for as long as I could stand it when she disappeared over the edge. But I came up empty. The current was strong that day. I'm a decent swimmer, but it nearly took me, too."

Ohmygod. Stifling a gasp, she said, "You jumped into an icy river to save your wife?"

The shame and horror of what she'd done to him punched her hard in the gut. Her eyes filled with tears, and her throat threatened to close. She couldn't breathe.

Thank heaven he turned away before he spoke again. "Not that it accomplished anything more than landing me in the hospital for a week, but yeah. I couldn't find her. Nothing I did…" His voice trailed off and he hung his head.

She reached out for him, desperate to apologize. Nearly frantic to take him in her arms and assuage his guilt, she fought her own tears.

Before she could touch his back, her better sense kicked in. There were many good reasons why she'd left the way she had. And those hadn't changed over the years. She fisted her hand, returned it to her side and took a step away from him.

Swallowing down the gigantic lump in her throat, she tried to find her balance. Something. She needed to *do* something. Or *say* something that would make him decide he'd been wrong about her and go away.

He turned around before she had her tears and nerves under control.

"Don't waste those tears on me," he whispered as he came closer. "I'm sorry I lost it like that. I never talk about the drowning. Never. It's just that you look so danged much like her. I…"

Say something, you idiot!

Shaking her head and sliding backward out of his space, she finally managed a coherent sentence. "Your story reminded me of the day my husband died in Iraq, I suppose. His tank unit was crossing a stream when they rolled over a roadside bomb. He drowned, never knowing he'd fathered a child, I'm afraid."

Sniffing loudly, she made a big show of wringing her hands and looking distraught.

Sympathy entered Gage's beautiful gray eyes and she took a deep breath. Thank goodness he'd bought her story. Now, she had to get away from him as fast as she could.

"I'd best be leaving now," she said briskly. "I'm traveling out of town. You just go on about your business. I'm not who you thought I was."

His eyes studied her carefully as he spoke. "But I wanted to know about the brooch in the window. You made it, right? Where'd you find that design?"

Oh, Lord. She'd forgotten all about that piece. "I created it, yes. But I don't remember finding that design anywhere. It's reminiscent of an Irish lace pattern my grandmother made."

"Well, my family's ranch has a brand that could be its twin. Seems odd to me that…"

"You must come from one of those big Western spreads, I'm thinking. Perhaps I saw your brand in a magazine long ago and it stayed buried in my head. I won't be selling the piece now."

With a slow shake of his head he sighed, but the questions still lingered in his expression. "The Bar-C has appeared in several magazine articles over the years. But…"

A great sadness gradually replaced the wariness in his eyes. "It doesn't matter if you sell it. I may buy it myself. I'm sorry if I scared you earlier."

"Seeing me just brought up all the old memories for you. Completely understandable. But I really must go now." She brushed past him and was out the back door before either her traitorous body or broken heart could make her change her mind.

She held the door open, waiting for him to take the hint

and walk away. He adjusted the ever-present cowboy hat and stepped out into the alley as she locked the door behind him.

A question came to her as she eased back and avoided getting too close to his muscled body. If he hadn't been looking for her, what the heck was he doing in Piñon Lake at this time of year?

"So, Mr. Chance…"

"Gage, please." He moved in on her as she backed herself up against the building.

"All right, Gage, then." Placing her purse in front of her chest as though to put away her key, she fended him off. "Uh, are you in Piñon Lake on vacation?"

"Business. Sort of."

"And is your business almost complete? Going home by Christmas, are you?"

He heaved a heavy sigh, then seemed to catch himself and rolled his shoulders under the heavy coat. "I've done what I came for. I'll be heading back to Texas now."

Nodding as though she understood, she tried a smile that only seemed to sear her heart with sadness. She remembered him using that same phrase—*Business. Sort of*—to describe what he did when he went searching for his lost little sister. So he was still looking. How sad. How terrible for him and his brothers.

The urge to say something to make him feel better almost finished her off. She couldn't. Couldn't let on that she understood the family's frustration of not knowing what had happened to their sister.

If he even suspected she knew more about him than she'd let on, he wouldn't stop. Just like he hadn't stopped looking for the little girl his family lost so tragically. He would hound her, never letting it rest, until he forced her to admit the truth.

Chancing a glance into his face, her pulse went wild

again. It raced as though they had been kissing. Oh, what she wouldn't give for another one of his passionate kisses.

Then she remembered the reason she couldn't kiss him and it made her stomach roll. Gage must stay safe. That thought was the only thing that had kept her going all this time.

She bid him goodbye and turned her back, walking down the frozen alley and hopefully out of his life for good. For the real truth was that she loved him. Desperately. And that would never change.

Silently, Gage watched her walk down the alley until her shape was only a shadow in the early morning light. After wallowing in the memories of Alicia's death and then falling into Elana's sad tale about her soldier husband's death, his brain had fogged over in utter misery.

He needed a drink and wondered if the bars were open yet. But the longer he stood still watching her walk, the more his mind began to clear. She walked with confidence, rather like Alicia. Confusion clogged his mind until curiosity bloomed instead. He didn't need a drink. He needed to have his head examined.

He must be losing brain cells. What the hell was the matter with him? Just being in her presence, looking at her, caused him to lose his mind?

He'd swallowed her story whole. Without a single question about why there was no trace of her or her daughter before she came to Piñon Lake. And why she had never once looked at him, a stranger who'd accosted her in an alley, with any fear in her eyes. He was definitely losing it.

Suddenly it all seemed like a scam. He'd been had somehow. Who the devil was she really?

Rushing down the alley after her retreating figure, he made up his mind to chase her to ground like he would chase down an errant calf. He would make her tell him the truth. Something, something big and desperate, lay behind those furtive glances and faraway looks. And he was determined to find out what it was.

Managing to keep her in sight, he followed her through the empty streets of town. At just after dawn, no one else had ventured out in the cold. She was moving fast, but he could have caught up to her anytime he wished.

Still, he waited. Walked and waited. Building huge possibilities in his mind as he went.

She was in hiding for reasons that could not be good. Mulling that over, he thought of her child and a knife-sharp pain twisted in his chest. He and Alicia had planned for a baby to come later, but her death put a stop to all those dreams.

This woman, this Elana Kelly, could not be his Alicia. But the similarities were startling. He suddenly needed to know more about her. Not entirely sure why he felt so determined, he just hated this confused feeling and needed something to make things clearer.

Moving after her, he felt shaken by the whole episode. By the time she finally reached a nearly empty parking lot at the edge of a residential area, he was running after her on a full head of steam. Answers. She would not get away until he had his answers.

She stopped beside an old three-door hatchback and dug in her purse like she was looking for keys. Before he made it to the car, she swung the door open and pitched her purse into the front seat.

"Stop!" Breathing hard from frustration and not from running, he grabbed her by the arm and tried to form words.

"Hey," she complained as she jerked her arm back. "Stop stalking me. Leave me alone."

He hung on to her wrist and managed to lower his voice

to the threatening purr he knew would keep her still. "Why? Why should I leave you alone? Who are you?"

Her eyes widened as she stopped struggling and slumped against the still open driver's side door. "Please…"

"I'm not leaving until you tell me the truth." He swallowed and steeled himself against the truth he expected to hear.

Suddenly she came to life again just when he thought she'd quit.

"Go away." Pounding her fists against his chest, she squirmed and twisted while tears flowed freely down her cheeks.

Not sure why, he only knew that his heart was breaking into a million pieces, watching her fight. This time her fear seemed clear enough. Fear of him. It killed him.

"Easy." He stepped closer and wrapped his arms around her as a way to keep her quiet. "I won't hurt you."

He wasn't sure whether she would believe him, but his words apparently sank in as she stopped fighting and rested her head against his chest. It was then that the scent of her finally reached his brain. The musky, clean smell that he'd dreamed about was clearly there. It clung to her and surrounded him with need just as it always had.

Thousands of memories bombarded him with sensual images of Alicia and him in an embrace exactly like this one. If he didn't move away from Elana now, he would be kissing her in the next minute.

Taking her by the shoulders, he gently set her away from him. "Elana, or whoever you are. You have to tell me the truth. I…"

His words were rudely interrupted by the telltale whoosh of a bullet whizzing by his head. It took him a precious second to react because it had been so sudden and the idea of being under attack came as such a surprise.

But he didn't stay still for long. "Someone's shooting at us. Move! Now!"

Chapter 3

"Watch it! I do not appreciate..." Elana couldn't finish her sentence due to Gage's rough treatment.

He pushed her into the car, never stopping until she went over the center console and landed in the passenger seat. Not her idea of a good time.

"Give me the keys. Hurry up." He climbed behind the wheel and held out his hand.

He had a lot of nerve. "This is my—"

"Someone. Is. Shooting at us!"

"Seriously?" She twisted to look around.

The pinging sound of something metallic hitting the fender close by her head finally got her attention. Throwing her keys at Gage, she ducked down below the side window.

"Buckle in," he said when her old hatchback came to life and he rammed it in gear.

She worked hard dragging the chest restraint over her body and locking down the buckle while still managing to stay hidden under the window of the careening car. But she accomplished it all as Gage raced out of the parking lot, driving like a maniac.

Muttering cuss words under his breath, he downshifted and made a quick right turn on to a side street. He gave the rearview mirror a quick check and then turned left at the next block. She could swear her ancient little four-wheel drive hatchback took the corner on two wheels.

"Are they following us?" She found herself practically screaming to be heard over the whine of the engine. "My car won't stand a lot of this kind of treatment."

Gage slowed at a stop sign and turned to her. "I saw a couple of guys get into a black pickup and start to follow us. But I think I lost them. Where are we?"

She glanced up through the windshield of the idling car to get her bearings. "On the east side of town. This little tourist trap only has about twenty streets total. Will they come looking for us, do you think?" Oops. She'd forgotten all about the phony Irish accent.

He didn't seem to notice. "That depends on why they were shooting at us. But generally when someone takes shots at you, it's meant to either scare or kill. If they wanted to kill us, they won't stop looking until they find us."

Swallowing hard, she fought the shakes that threatened to bounce her right out of her seat. "We need to hide, then."

"Or run, yeah, I agree." He took his foot off the brake, pressed on the clutch and eased out onto a busier street.

"Why?" She was fast becoming sick to her stomach.

"Why what? Why would someone shoot at us?"

Still fighting the nausea, she nodded without saying a word.

He set his jaw and his knuckles whitened on the steering wheel. "I haven't the foggiest idea. But people don't just go around shooting at other people at six in the morning for no reason. They had to have followed us or else how would they have known where to find us? Which means they've been stalking one of us. And if they went to all that trouble, they'll keep looking until they find us again."

"But…" Her mind raced as she tried to stem the panic. "We must hide the car."

"I have a better idea." He swung the wheel and made a U-turn in the middle of the block. "As long as we stay out of their sight until we get there, my hotel has an underground parking garage. That's the best place I can think of to hide the car for now. Unless you have somewhere else in mind?"

Shaking her head, she sank back down in the seat as far as possible. She didn't want to hide. She needed to get the heck out of town. But Gage couldn't know her true intentions. He would just follow her. And she couldn't let him do that.

Glancing over at him, she saw the deep concentration clearly set across his features. How had he become involved in her life again so fast? And why now?

Maybe at the hotel she'd find a way to sneak away from him, leave her car and take the town shopping shuttle back to Brendan's. He would trade cars with her temporarily so she could make her way out of town yet today.

Yes, that was the plan. All she needed to do was wait for her opportunity. And not say too much to Gage in the meantime. He had a way of making her say—and do—things she never would have done before him.

The larger streets of town started filling up with cars and taxis as the sun finally rose over the eastern mountain peaks. That should warm the air. But nothing could warm her insides. She was in a frozen panic. Wrapping her arms around her upper body to stem the chills, she prayed they would reach the hotel without being spotted.

In the next block, Gage suddenly dragged at the wheel

and took a quick left into a back alley. There was barely room enough to navigate through the tiny space.

"What's going on?" she demanded. "We've only one long block to go before we arrive at the hotel."

"I saw the same truck again." He slowed and stopped in a deep shadow behind a three-story building. "I hope they didn't spot us."

Elana was panting like she'd just run a mile. "Perhaps we should stay right here for a while. Until they give up, that is."

"Get this through your head. They are not likely to give up. But…" he added with a wary glare, "it'll be okay for us to stay here for a few minutes and hope they start looking across town. We only need enough time and space to drive to the hotel."

Time. Time to ask questions? Big mistake. She had a feeling she knew what would be coming next.

Sure enough, he said, "In the meantime we can talk."

She needed to come up with something else fast. "It wouldn't be a good idea for us to stay here for that long, I'm guessing." Opening her door, she began fumbling with her seat belt buckle. "Let's leave the car and walk to the hotel, then. They won't be expecting us to be on foot."

Darned belt buckle jammed. Frantic, she tugged at the stupid contraption.

Next thing she knew, Gage laid a hand on her shoulder. "Stop," he murmured gently. "Wait a few moments. We'd be easy targets if they spotted us walking."

Flopping back against the seat, she uttered a heavy sigh and gave up her struggle.

Oh, Gage. You were always two steps ahead of me. Why did I ever think I could outrun you?

Watching Elana send furtive glances around in every direction made him want to gather her in his arms and protect her from the danger. He hadn't felt like this about anyone since before Alicia had died.

But she wasn't Alicia. At least, he didn't think so. Still, the minute he'd seen her, the old combination of lust and longing got tangled up with the grief and anger he'd felt over his wife's death.

"So, who would want to shoot at you?" He tried to keep the tension out of his voice. "You have enemies you'd like to tell me about? Someone trying to frighten you?"

For a split second a look of pure terror filled her eyes, then it was gone again just as fast.

"Me? There haven't been any troubles in my life. Not until you showed up, that is. Whoever the shooter is, he must've been aiming at you."

Straightening her shoulders into a hard line, she went on, "Which adds up to the best reason I can think of for why I should be on my own. As soon as we reach the safety of the hotel, I'll be finding another way home. I'd be far better off alone and can send someone for the car later."

"Give me a second to think." Gage sat back, studying her profile while keeping one eye on their surroundings.

Everything she'd said was probably a lie. His gut screamed at him not to trust anything coming from her mouth. This whole picture felt wrong. Besides, something undefined was nagging at his subconscious. But he'd been so taken with Elana's resemblance to Alicia and then the shooting that he couldn't put his finger on what was wrong.

Was this his Alicia? But how could that be?

His first impulse involved shaking the truth out of her. But that meant a return to those conflicting emotions again. Still, something terrible lurked right behind that innocent, irate look on her face. Even though his mind was still laden with confusion, he'd never been more positive of anything in his life. The woman was terrified.

Keeping his anger and grief bottled up, at least long enough to make her give him the truth, would be the smartest course of action. He could keep the nasty sentiments to himself, and bury them so deep she would never suspect.

Ever since his days as a young orphaned teen, isolated at school and miserable over the bullying he'd endured, he had learned the value of keeping his emotions under wraps. Add to those years of training the five long years of grief he'd spent since Alicia's death, and he'd become an expert at disguising what was in his mind and heart.

Anger was definitely his most destructive emotion. Anger got him nowhere and he needed to keep at least that one emotion tightly controlled.

Looking at her, watching her trying hard to keep her fear at bay, he thought controlling his anger would be an especially smart idea around Elana. At least while other emotions bounced around inside him like Ping-Pong balls.

Protectiveness.

Grief.

Need.

Lust.

It was hard enough to look at her and not want to take her in his arms.

Every time she tilted her head just so or sighed in that special way, he was reminded enough of the wife who'd haunted his dreams for five years that he had to stop himself from reliving the pain of her death over and over. Alicia was gone for good. He'd watched her go into the water. She had to be gone.

Even as her mirror image sat right beside him. Was Elana a relative? A relative in terrible trouble?

"Well? Have you thought it over, then?" She turned her head to face him. "We've been in one spot for too long. Will you let me go?"

"No." He started the car and carefully pulled out of their hiding place. "Keep your eyes open and look for that black truck."

Just like one of Alicia's expressions, her face gave away her frustration. But to her credit, Elana didn't whine or try to cajole him into changing his mind. Instead, she offered the best driving route for reaching the relative safety of the underground parking from the alley.

Two quick turns later and he used his card key so they could enter the hotel's underground lot. "We'll park as close as we can. I wish my rental was in this lot, too. But I parked it in the back lot yesterday."

"Could we just change vehicles and never go inside?" Her eyes were narrowed on him but the look on her face said she knew what she was talking about.

Sounding very much like somebody accustomed to using escape techniques, she'd managed to make him even more curious. Oh, yeah. They were going to have a very long conversation. Just as soon as he found them someplace quiet—and safe—to talk.

"I intend to retrieve my weapon and money from the hotel safe first. Get out."

Unbuckling as he pocketed her keys, she looked up with her eyebrows raised. "You have a gun?"

"Yeah. I have a license to carry."

He watched her swallow hard and then try to cover her fear by relaxing her expression. "I have a small overnighter case in the back. I want to take it with me."

Images raced through his mind at her choice of words. *Overnighter.* Long, sensual nights full of her, body and soul, came back as pictures to haunt him. With all the time in the world to explore every sensitive nook and cranny of each other's body, they'd made the most of the number of nights allotted to them together before his wife had been ripped from his arms. He had a year's worth of sensual pictures stored up of making love to her.

But those weren't the images he needed in his head right now. What he most needed to remember was that the woman in front of him was obviously running from something. From him? Maybe. More likely from the person or persons who took shots at them.

Just what kind of people had she been involved with? Were they from her past? And who the heck was this woman, really? Did he want her to be his dead wife? Or would he rather not have to face that much deception from someone he'd been sure had loved him?

"Fine," he said as he came around the car to stand beside the hatchback's door.

She could have her overnighter, but he would keep a close eye on her. No telling what that bag held. Could be anything. A sexy nightgown. Or a .38 special.

With her duffel over her shoulder, Elana led Gage through the lot and into the hotel's lobby, her mind racing the whole time. There had to be a way to lose him in the busy hotel.

At least now she was positive he hadn't deliberately led her father or ex-fiancé to her hiding spot. He'd been in the line of fire the same as her. It still seemed too highly coincidental that he'd found her by accident. But she didn't have time to reason out an answer to that problem.

When they entered the hotel's main lobby area, she looked around, desperate for some way out. *He* had no idea what kind of menace they were up against. But *she* did. The only way to save him was to run again.

And leave him far behind. That's why she'd done everything. All of it. And why she would keep on trying to confuse the issue, making him think he'd brought the trouble with him.

Dear God, why hadn't her disappearance worked the first time? Why wasn't Gage safe and sound at home in Texas with his family? She wanted to wring his neck. Or kiss him senseless. Either. Both.

Forcing the useless regrets out of her mind so she could concentrate on a plan, Elana narrowed her gaze on every corner of the wide-open lobby. Straight ahead lay the main registration desk and offices, flanked by the concierge and bellman's desk. To the left was a narrow corridor that led to the elevator bank, the public phones and the back entrance to the lobby. To the right was the wide-open space containing a small news and notion store along with the large, casual-dining restaurant, the only place to eat in the hotel.

As she watched, more and more people arrived at the restaurant desk, waiting to be seated for breakfast. The place began to swarm with people. She made a mental note not to be caught out in the open near those crowds. No, the other, more quiet and isolated way would be a better route for escape.

Think, she chided herself. How was she going to lose Gage and not be seen by their stalkers? They couldn't get close enough to identify him. She'd been so careful over the years to keep him out of her past problems. And she intended to keep things that way.

Her best chance for disappearing would be while he retrieved his things from the hotel office's safe. If she had enough time, she could take an elevator to an upper floor before he knew which direction she'd gone. Then after a good period of time, she'd sneak back down via the stairs and slip outside by the employee entrance. She'd be able to walk home from here. Brendan would help.

Good plan. Or as good as she was likely to get in the next few minutes. She set her mind on the idea.

Her senses went on hyper-alert as Gage dragged her along

with him across the lobby toward the main desk. The skin prickled at the back of her neck.

"This may not be such a good idea," she whispered to him as they approached one of the office managers. "It's too public here, to my mind."

"We're only going to take a few moments. Keep still."

The office manager asked how he could help. When Gage told him, Elana prepared to make a run for the elevators.

"I'll wait for you here, then," she said with a phony smile plastered in place.

"Oh, no, you don't." Gage grabbed her hand and pulled her close to his body. Close enough to feel the warmth of him right through his winter clothes. "Stick with me. We'll be done and on our way soon enough."

There went her terrific plan of escape. Now what? She decided to wait and stay alert.

They followed the manager to the hotel's bank of safety deposit boxes. The manager left them alone and she fidgeted while Gage went through the motions of cleaning out his box.

When they came back out into the main lobby, her whole body trembled with the sure knowledge that trouble stalked them—close by. "What now?"

"We'll head out the back entrance." Gage turned toward the elevators while she tried to make herself invisible by hiding behind his broad shoulders.

Suddenly, he halted his steps.

"What's the matter?"

"It's them. Coming in the same way we did. Stay behind me."

Elana wholeheartedly agreed with him. She was the one they were after. Maybe the two of them could still get out of the hotel without being overtaken.

"Uh-oh." Gage swung around, wrapping an arm around

her waist as he went. "They spotted us and they're headed
in our direction. We have to find another way."

"But…" They'd recognized him, too? How?

He didn't stop to explain but made a direct line toward
the busy restaurant, moving so fast his body carried her
along with his momentum.

The wrong way. "But all these people," she tried to say.

"Stick with me." He barged in front of the long line of
customers and met with a lot of grumbled complaints. The
hostess tried to stop him from entering the restaurant, but
he dashed around her.

"We're meeting someone," he called over his shoulder
while dancing through the busy tables.

Checking behind them as they ran, she saw a couple of
big, dark men in heavy suits trying to follow in their wake
through the irritated crowds. Those guys definitely had the
look of the Russian mob about them. A chill went up her
spine.

"We're in trouble." She tried to make him listen but he
was heading for the back of the restaurant as fast as he could
go. "Gage, wait. We need to call the police. We're trapped."

Next thing she knew, he burst through the door to the
kitchen and ran right into a waitress carrying two armloads
of trays. Plates, food, glasses and water crashed around them
with a dreadful clamor. Elana nearly slipped on the mess,
but Gage never slowed down, still dragging her with him.

"This way." He pushed past the cooks working at their
stations.

People called after them. Everyone was yelling. But Gage
still never slowed. He shoved one guy to the floor who'd
tried to stop them.

"Sorry," he mumbled as he left the poor man in their dust.

All of a sudden they crashed through another door and

found themselves in the open air on a loading dock. To the left was a ramp to the ground.

"Let's go." Gage found the right door and in moments they were blessedly in the parking lot, running full-out.

He pulled a key fob from his pants pocket and beeped opened the doors to a black SUV on the fly. "Get in!"

Buckling in while he started the engine and hit the gas, she turned to look behind them. Just as they were about to leave the parking lot, the two men who'd been chasing them came out on the dock and pointed in their direction.

Busted. "They've seen us."

"Just keep your head down. They still have to catch us."

But she knew these men. Or ones like them. And knew that they would never stop. They would catch up. Sooner or later.

Chapter 4

After doubling back on their tracks several times to be sure no one was following, Gage drove them to one of the picturesque ski resort hotels a few miles north in the mountains. Tired and hungry and in no mood to deal with more of her lies, he figured Elana—or whoever she was—would talk to him, tell him why she had no past and who was chasing her, if only they could spend a few hours in quiet so he could gain her trust.

The first resort he came to seemed new but made to look like one of the Sierras' oldest lodge hotels. With four multi-levels and a stone facade, the place was too kitschy for his taste, but it would do for what he needed.

He pulled into the hotel's covered lot and parked. "We're going in. Bring your duffel."

She stared over at him. "I'm not staying with you. Let me go. Perhaps if we separate, we'll have a better chance of escape."

The fury suddenly erupted inside him like a volcano, leaving him incapable of speech. Silently repeating his vow to keep his anger under control, he ripped the key from the ignition and stepped out of the SUV.

In two seconds he'd flung her door open and had her by the arm. "Get out." He knew his voice was too low, too full of danger, but he couldn't help it. "We've come this far. You owe me—" he bit off the anger, tried to calm down "—explanations. You will at least tell me why those men are after you."

She glared at him but swung her feet out of the SUV and slid to the ground. "I don't know you. And I don't owe you any explanations."

"Oh, yes, you do. Those men are after me, too, now." He jerked her close, made sure he picked up her overnighter and headed to registration.

But as he walked them toward the hotel lobby, the earthy scent coming from her body took his imagination on a trip down memory lane. Pictures of his fingers stroking along the sensitive skin of Alicia's lush breasts bombarded his mind, leaving him breathless. The echoed feel of her long legs entwined around his waist or his palms cupping her rounded bottom seemed so real that his fingers twitched and his heart pounded.

"Are you okay?" Her voice, and the Irish tinge behind it, woke him up to the idea that he was still confused about who he was saving.

"Fine. Just fine." Was this the woman he'd spent endless nights making love to?

Not possible. But then who was she?

He marched them through the nearly empty lobby, with its pretentious restaurant, spa and boutique stores, toward the registration desk. She struggled to stay behind when he approached the man on duty behind the fake stone desk.

"Oh, no, you don't," he growled in her ear. "We're in this together."

"Yes, sir. Do you need a room?" The clerk had a smile plastered on his face that was as phony as the potted plant on the counter.

"My wife and I will only be staying the night."

Elana's muffled complaint to his remarks died in her throat. Good thing. He would've hated having to explain to the complete stranger behind the desk why he'd all but kidnapped her.

"You're in luck, sir. We've had one cancellation for a king room this evening. There's a snowboard competition being held on the slopes this week and we're booked solid. Now, if you wanted to stay over until Christmas Eve…"

"No need. One night will do it."

It took a few moments for the clerk to sign them in and turn over the card keys. As they left the desk, Elana held out her hand.

"What?"

"A key. The clerk gave you two. One of them is for me."

"Forget it." Gage dragged her to the elevator and pushed the up button. "You're not leaving my sight."

Folding her arms over her chest, she pouted as they rode the elevator to the third floor. His emotions kept running the gamut from simmering lust to instant fury. He couldn't find balance.

With her in tow, he stormed the empty upstairs hallway to their room in utter silence. One word from her and he would've exploded. Or he would have taken her right here in the hall. But she seemed to know that and stayed quiet.

Once inside their room, he threw her duffel on the enormous bed and locked the door behind them. "Stay put." He shucked his hat and coat. "I'll check the bathroom."

Keeping one eye on her as she paced the large room, he

double-checked the space to be sure they were alone. After he was satisfied, he came back and settled into a chair at the small, round table by the window.

"Sit," he ordered.

Glaring at him, she remained standing.

Forcing her to do as he wished would get him nowhere. He wanted her to trust him so they could talk honestly.

"Are you hungry?"

She pressed her lips together and set her jaw.

"Well, I am. How about I order us some sandwiches? Or maybe a pizza?"

Without uttering a word, she turned and walked across the room to stare out the window.

Shrugging, he kept talking to her while he picked up the house phone to place an order. "I get really hungry for pizza. We don't have any pizza joints in the small town where I come from. Or maybe you remember that?"

He watched her back stiffen, but she made no comment. It had been worth a shot. Not that he really thought this was Alicia. Not really. It couldn't be.

Still, any kind of direct assault probably wasn't the way to go about making her trust him enough for the truth. This situation called for a little finesse.

He got lucky. The hotel's restaurant had ten-minute pizza delivery on the menu. He ordered a large pepperoni pizza and sodas. He might've liked a beer but figured both of them needed to keep their heads today.

"Please sit down." He wasn't above pleading. "I really need your help so we can devise a plan to get out of this mess."

It was easy to visualize her weakening resolve just by the slump of her body. Finally, she removed her coat and placed it on the back of a chair, then sat across from him. But she said not one word the whole time.

Racking his brain for some way to break the tension and begin to develop trust, the start of an idea just popped out of his mouth. "You don't have a phone with you, do you?"

She shook her head and folded her hands on the table.

"I bet you think cell phones are too easy to hack, right?" Nothing. No response. Not even a blink.

"You might be right. But I have my satellite phone with me. You want to call and check on your daughter?"

The look in her eyes said it all. Relief. And then respect. At last she said, "Yes, please."

Grabbing his coat, he dug out the phone and handed it to her. "Whoever you contact, I would like to suggest you don't tell them exactly where we are. You're safe with me here for the time being. But not if word leaks out."

She nodded and he actually believed she wouldn't say anything. Why he thought that was beyond him. The woman was obviously a liar—and heaven only knew what else she was. Maybe a criminal.

But after she punched in a number on his phone, he figured that at least *one* of them was going to learn how to trust today. She spoke to someone on the line in what had to be Gaelic and then spoke quietly in English. He would just have to hope she hadn't betrayed them.

The pizza arrived just as she hung up.

He doled out slices to each of them and then sat at the table and dug in.

After she hung up, he swallowed a bite and said, "This is pretty good. Have a piece before it gets cold."

Elana tilted her head but made no move to eat. "I'll be thanking you for allowing me to talk to my child. She was concerned, but I believe I calmed her down."

"So she's okay?"

"Temporarily. She's caught the gist of the grown-ups' concern over my situation, I'm guessing. Kids can see the true picture, not so much from words but from the attitudes of people around them. Plus, my baby had to leave her home today. I tried turning it into a game, but she's so smart. I imagine she knows something is very wrong."

He was suddenly struck by the fact that whatever else she was, Elana was a mother first. "I'm sorry."

"Don't be. It's not your fault, then." Absently, she picked at the edge of her pizza slice.

Not so hesitant, he reached for another slice and had half of it in his mouth before something happened that made him nearly choke on it.

Watching her, he was stunned when she daintily stripped off the piece of pepperoni on her slice and popped the meat into her mouth first. Exactly the way Alicia used to do. How many women in the world would eat pizza that same way? Maybe millions. Maybe only one.

While gulping most of a can of soda in order to calm down, he came to the decision not to call her on the obvious tell. But he was becoming ever more confused by the moment. Could this woman actually be his Alicia? If she was, he had a lot more questions. Like *why* she wore a disguise and why the ruse of her death? Meanwhile, the ache in the vicinity of his heart became overpowering.

"So, I guess that means you're ready to admit those guys are after you and not me?" He had to hope that didn't sound too pushy.

It wasn't the real question he wanted answered. But it was a start.

"I am, yes." Honest at least, she finished off her slice and reached for another.

"Well, since I'm in this with you up to my Stetson, do you mind telling me why they'd want to hurt you—an innocent Iraqi war widow?"

"It would be a long story."

The cheese string between her mouth and her hand drew out into a long line. Focusing on the offending cheese, he couldn't help himself; he had to touch her mouth. Breaking the string with one swipe, he let his fingers linger on her lips. Her tongue slipped out and licked, and his pulse spiked.

Quickly he withdrew and grabbed his soda can again. "We have time. Tell me."

For a minute she looked shell-shocked, as if his touch had electrified her the same as it had done to him. Then she recovered and replaced the panic with a blasé look.

Elana chastised herself. She'd tried to remain aloof but Gage was making it impossible. He had probably saved her life back in town and she'd treated him so shabbily through all of this. He hadn't ever deserved the pain she'd caused him. But nothing had changed. She had to find a way to keep him out of harm.

An idea hit her. If she came up with a bad enough story, maybe she could make him hate her. Then he would be sure to leave her alone and go back to Texas where he'd be safe.

"You'll have to understand the way I was raised, then," she began. "The family traditions and…my heritage."

"Okay. Were you born in another country?"

She looked down at the table. "In Ireland, yes. But since moving here, we don't participate in American life."

It was his turn to shake his head and shrug a shoulder. "Explain."

This would be only a partial a lie. She rarely gave up her real background because she knew what people's reactions would be. In this case she hoped he would be disgusted enough to let her go. For his own sake.

"We are Rom—*gypsies* to you. My long-ago ancestors moved from Romania to Ireland."

"A gypsy?" The look of astonishment on his face was

exactly the reason she hadn't ever wanted to tell him the truth when they'd been married.

In most people she met, after the astonishment wore off, hostility usually came next. She dreaded seeing an expression of prejudice on Gage's face. So she didn't look at him.

Pouring herself a soda, she noticed her hand shaking as she tipped the can to her glass. "We do things differently than the norm, I'm thinking. Actually, not the same as any other people on earth. We don't assimilate. Rom don't want to be like everyone else."

At least that's what her father always told her. She'd never been quite as positive that living outside the mainstream was the best thing for everyone.

"Gypsies." He said it as though the word itself was dirty. "Were you raised to travel around? To keep moving from place to place?"

She couldn't look up at him while answering. "That is our heritage, yes. But most of today's generations put down at least temporary roots. Here in America, anyway."

"But even if you've settled here, your other traditions are...unusual. Right?"

"Very." She wondered how bad she could make this sound. Bad enough to make him walk away?

"I hate to sound...um...biased." His voice had a hesitation in it she'd seldom heard from him. "But the only thing I remember reading about gypsies, other than the traveling, was about how they're criminals. Or at least small-time crooks."

Heat flamed her cheeks, so she ducked her head and tsked at him. "That's painting millions of people with a broad and unkind brush." Unfortunately, in her family's case, it was all too true. But she couldn't let him think that about the entire race of people.

"Today gypsies are more likely to run small businesses or work in the trades. We don't like to talk about ourselves, and I suppose that tradition of silence makes us seem like criminals to *some* people. And...uh..." She had to make this sound bad. "Hate to admit this, but in my family, it's mostly true."

"You're not kidding about this, are you?"

She only wished this was one big joke. "I'll not be lying, thank you."

Gage was staring at her as though he was seeing some piece of garbage that had washed up from the depths of the ocean. This, this look of contempt and confusion on his face, was only one of the reasons she'd never told him even this much of her story before.

As she swallowed the last of the liquid in her glass, she decided on another half-truth. Mixing truth with falsehood came easy to her. Anything she could do to save him from himself.

Folding her arms around her middle to keep steady, she began, "You see, when I was fifteen, my parents arranged a marriage to a Rom boy that I had never met."

"Were you upset about the idea? What'd you think of having to marry a man your parents chose?" Gage had scooted his chair back, too, and now leaned his elbows on his knees. His look of concern and confusion made her want to smooth her fingers over the creases on his beautiful face.

It suddenly hit her how much she'd missed touching this wonderful man.

Deliberately, she balled her fists and shook her head, letting out all the weariness that had built up over the last day. "I'd known for my whole life that an arranged marriage would be in my future. It bothered me a bit that I had never even met the boy. I assumed I had little choice."

She laughed at little at how stupid that sounded now.

Still her story had to move on and go downhill from here. "But I was the smart kid in my family and my father had let me continue with school. So by the time I was fifteen, I'd had far too much education to just accept the situation completely."

Unable to watch Gage while lying about the rest, she stood and looked out the window as the lavender light of twilight threw dusk's shadows across the slopes. "When I was nearing the age to marry, I deliberately went out and found myself a non-gypsy guy who was willing to take me away. He wasn't all that bright. But he was nice enough."

She turned in time to see the frown lines developing across Gage's face even through the growing darkness. Good. Maybe he would finally give up trying to save her.

"You never loved this guy?" He looked hurt, as though he thought she was talking about him. "You just used him?"

Forcing herself to give him a sly smile, she nodded. "Sure. I figured I would give him a few months and then just disappear."

All of a sudden it occurred to her how this might sound to Gage. She hadn't meant for her story to come anywhere close to their situation. This was just a story. Not *their* story.

On the other hand, that might not be such a bad idea if it would make him leave. "I mean, yeah, I know I'm a terrible person. But what can you expect?"

She tried to keep her voice calm as she turned back to the window and changed the subject as if what she'd said meant nothing. "Let's leave the lights off in here. Do you mind? They'll be lighting the slopes soon for the competition. That should throw off enough of a glow for us to see if we leave the curtains open. I want to be able to see outside."

She needed to remain composed and darkness had a way of hiding her true feelings. Staying calm and cool, cool enough to say the exact right thing to drive him away, was all that mattered now.

"All right." His quick agreement was amicable. Maybe too amicable.

She needed to put distance between them. So out of the blue, she yawned and stretched, hoping he would take the hint and go.

"You look tired," he said softly. "Why don't you lie down for a while? I'll stand guard. Finish your story later. I'm not going anywhere."

Chapter 5

"What'd you say?" The room's ambient lighting was enough for Gage to see something like panic spreading across her face. "Why won't you just leave? I'll be okay."

"I'm not leaving you in danger. I don't care what you've done in the past. It doesn't matter. You have a child now and I believe you've become a decent person. I'll see this through to the end."

He'd said the words, but frustration at not knowing if she was Alicia and had been talking about him in her story, burned in his gut. The person she'd been describing as her younger self was not at all the person he'd thought he'd known as his wife. She couldn't be that person. He didn't care what she'd said.

But he wasn't ready for an argument. His mind was too jumbled. He knew his body—his senses and his libido—felt the same way about this woman as it had about his wife. Still, his mind was fairly sure the two women were not the same.

Holding up both hands, palms out, he tried soothing words. "Take it easy. It shouldn't be a terrible hardship to have me around. I think I've proven I can be handy in emergencies."

"Uh... I don't know." She walked over to sit on the bed in an effort that seemed designed to keep her as far away from him as possible.

But her simple moves turned him hard and ready in an instant. The situation seemed crazy as all hell. If she was Alicia, he should hate her. And if she wasn't... Well, he shouldn't be having these protective urges toward her. Nor should he be experiencing the most arousing desire he'd felt in over five years. From the moment he'd seen her, he'd wanted her.

He'd tried to move on with his social life since Alicia's death, had even endured a few fix-ups by his brothers. But no one else electrified him with one look. No other women made him crave, lust uncontrollably, or lit him with such a fiery passion in such a short time.

No, only this one. And only because she reminded him of his dead wife? Crazy.

"Forget everything for now," he said as soothingly as he could manage as he inched toward her. "Don't think about it. Try to get some rest. You can decide what's best later. I'll be right here."

Just then the floodlights went on outside and doused the room in a warm glow. She made a strangled noise in her throat and he put a hand on her shoulder.

She turned to look up at him. "No one can see us, can they?"

The husky sound of her voice. The sudden blazing desire in her deep green eyes combined with that sincere look of tenderness. Everything about her produced such a drastic change in the atmosphere of the room around them that he could barely move.

And all of it saturated him with such an acute wanting that he couldn't catch his breath.

He cleared his throat and eased down to sit beside her. "No. You were right the first time. We can see out. But we're too far away from the slopes, and without the room's back-lighting it won't be possible to see in here from the grounds even with the curtains open."

She looked over at him and the expression in her eyes went straight to his gut. Damn.

The eye color wasn't right. The hair color wasn't right. Even the voice wasn't the same. But that erotic look she'd given him and that intimate warmth were all Alicia.

"Do you have a family?" she whispered, while pinning him with another tender look full of longing.

He couldn't manage an answer. Conflicting emotions choked him, threatened to leave him a whimpering fool.

I don't care who you are. Love me. Be mine. If only for tonight.

Low, gravelly words finally scraped out of his mouth. "Family. Yes. Brothers and sisters-in-law. Their kids. And my aunt."

"No significant other? No one since your wife died?"

"I've tried…" he admitted reluctantly. "But sometimes being with someone when it's not right is worse than being alone."

He didn't expect her to understand.

"I know what you mean." And when he gazed into her eyes, he could see that she meant every word.

Dang, he wanted her desperately. Was it just because of the resemblance to his lost wife? What if they did make love and he ran across differences? In her body. In the way she made love. There were bound to be differences.

Could he stand to take that chance?

Sighing, she reached over and took his face in her hands. Forced to gaze deep into those dark green eyes again, he spotted a surprisingly empathetic sheen covering them.

"I need a hug. And you do, too, I'm thinking." Sliding her arms around him, she leaned in and pressed him close.

It was too much. He couldn't deny her. His arms came up, capturing her lush body as she melted into him.

God, this was such a good idea. Shutting his eyes, he let himself go, inhaling her achingly familiar scent and reveling in her precious warmth. Leaning his head against the satin of her hair, he dreamed of another Christmas—long ago and far away.

Then, she turned her face and her lips brushed against his. His body responded, growing hard and pulsing with need. He wanted her, whoever she was, with a sudden heat that threatened to overwhelm them both.

God, this was such a bad idea. But knowing that he might get hurt later didn't much matter. Not now.

With his body throbbing, he took the kiss deeper. Her mouth was hungry. Hot. Wet. Wild. He swept his tongue inside her parted lips and tasted everything that reminded him of home.

Lordy mercy, but the woman could kiss. The deep humming groan, coming from low in her throat, told him she was every bit as turned on as he was. It took him back to the last time he and Alicia had blow-your-socks-off sex. Fantastic. Addictive. He remembered and his body responded as it always had. And he craved more—and more.

His groans matched hers as he pulled back slightly and filled his hands with her breasts. "Alicia, darlin'."

She let out a small sob as she gave his chest a halfhearted shove. "This can't happen. Please."

He dropped his hands and shook his head to come out of the haze. "Sorry. I shouldn't have…" Standing, he hung his head and tried to douse the flames.

The two women weren't that much alike. But this one turned him on, and that was dangerous.

"No. It was mostly my fault," she said wearily. "I'm just so tired—and scared. I think I'm going out of my mind."

What was the matter with him? Here he was, taking advantage of a vulnerable woman in a tough situation. It rocked him to think he'd become a bully of the worst sort. He could barely stand to look at her now.

"Lie back and take that rest," he said in the gentlest voice he could find, though it still sounded strangled. "We'll finish our talk and look for a way out of here in a few hours. After the competition on the slopes. In the meantime, you might as well try to sleep."

"I don't think I can," she argued. But she leaned against the pillows and closed her eyes.

He reached for a blanket and pulled it up over her legs. "There you go. I'll keep watch so you don't have to worry. Just close your eyes and relax."

He moved around to the other side of the bed. "I'll be right here." Sitting on the bed, he kicked off his boots and rested his back against the headboard. "I'll wake you if anything happens."

Stupid. He should've known from the beginning this was not his deceased wife. In the entire time they'd been together, Alicia had never once shown any sign of fear or vulnerability. Her take-no-guff-from-anyone attitude was something that had made him curious, but he'd just assumed it came from being without a family for so long.

Elana was different. She reminded him of himself as a

young boy. Back then he'd felt like an outcast even with a large family—lost when his mother had been murdered and his father wrongly sent to prison for the crime. His two older brothers, both also young, had been so busy trying to hold things together and support a ranch and six kids that they'd ended up ignoring the emotional needs of the rest of them.

He glanced over, admiring Elana's peaceful face while she slept. So beautiful in the warm glow of light streaming through the window. Underneath her vulnerable exterior, had she come from the same place he'd come from?

Had Elana broken free of her family in the same too-forceful manner as he had on that long ago day when the bullies at school taunted him one time too many? He'd been so vulnerable back then, timid and alone while rumors spread like wildfire during the trial, giving the other kids lots of fodder to tease. According to rumor, his father had supposedly run the ranch into the ground. More, the word was he'd been cheating on his wife until the day she caught him in the act. None of it was true, but every word was like barbed wire to a young Gage's injured heart.

He'd remained silent through everything. Not wanting to burden his brothers any more than they already were. He was the good boy. The one that never gave anyone any trouble.

But he remembered the final straw like it was yesterday. His rolling emotions, the fear of being alone and the un-released grief from losing his beloved mother, broke free that day and he'd sprung at the boy who'd been the worst bully of them all. No one could separate them and the fight turned ugly. When it was done, the other boy, bloodied and broken, had to be taken to the hospital. Gage was expelled.

That was when his aunt June came back to Chance and moved in. She tutored him for the remainder of the year and then convinced the principal that he'd repented and changed so he could enter high school the next year.

Meanwhile, his father was sentenced to life in prison, a younger brother died in a ranching accident, his sister had been kidnapped and his oldest brother had joined the army. But Gage never felt shy or vulnerable again. Breaking free had made him tough. And he'd made the decision that seeking justice and protection for others less fortunate would be his life's mission.

Elana moaned in her sleep and he felt her fear like a living thing. Leaning over, he pulled her close to his chest and let his body heat along with his solemn promise of protection seep into her even as she slept. He would never let any harm come to her.

She might not be Alicia, but she was a woman in trouble. That's all he needed to know.

Elana's subconscious mind lifted her back to a Christmas from long ago on the wings of a dream.

The Austin night was as cold as the day had been long. She'd met Gage for a late night supper in a quaint bistro near the river.

"How was your day?" he asked as he reached for her hand across the table.

"Boring without you." That was the truth but the lies tripped easily off her tongue for the rest of the conversation. "I toured the state capitol, did a little shopping and walked across the university's campus.

"How was your day?" she asked brightly. "How's the case coming?"

Gage grinned at her and began the retelling of how he'd almost wrapped up his case by getting a line on the man who'd scammed an elderly woman out of her retirement account. Elana sipped her wine and nodded in all the appropriate places.

She was almost ready. After carefully laying down the

clues for her husband to find so he could crack his case and put the Russian mobster responsible for this scam behind bars, she'd spent the rest of the day making her own plans.

Out of time, she knew she couldn't spend even one more wonderful night with Gage. Meeting him here in public was pushing the envelope, but she'd had to see him. Had to set up the scenario for her accidental drowning scene.

"You are so beautiful," he murmured as he leaned over and seared a kiss across her lips. "I can't wait to get you back to the hotel room."

How was she ever going to do without him? He was the most sensual man she'd ever met. And the most plainly decent human being she knew. The last year with him had changed her. Made her wish she could be the person he thought she was.

Because of his influence, she'd even changed her ways enough to secretly help solve his investigations. After being one of them, she understood the Texas underworld crowd and knew where to point the clues, something she'd never thought she would do.

But what if there were no lies between them? How would their lives be different then?

Sighing, she smiled at him across the table while thinking that it was just as well she'd begun their relationship with lies. Gage had a strong knight-in-shining-armor complex and would want to protect her instead of running from the danger. Silly man. Regular people just aren't capable of standing their ground against an all-powerful and unseen enemy.

This morning that point had been brought home to her with a bang. As she'd carefully planted the last clue to lead Gage and the police to their man, she'd been spotted by the very Russians she left behind long before she met and married him.

She was well aware of what being seen by those creeps meant. It was time to go again. Start another new life. She'd thought of going to Gage for help, but she couldn't let him get involved in her danger or he might die trying to save her. So she'd come up with a plan to die first.

But she was still devastated about not having him in her life after tonight. It hurt just to consider living without him. Hurt so badly that she couldn't think about it right now.

Instead, while they ate their light bistro meal, she let her mind take her back to last night. The last night they would ever have together.

He'd ordered room service so they could spend more time in bed, and that had been fine by her. Being with Gage was all the sustenance her body needed. She'd thought she might starve without him.

"Here you go, darlin'." He fed her the last of a chocolate chip cookie while nuzzling her neck.

Man sure knew how to get her back into bed.

Hooking her arms around his neck, she pressed her hips against his and rocked. Which was all the invitation he needed. He raised his head and kissed her, with those amazing lips of his blazing hot trails and tasting twice as spicy as their meal.

The fireworks between them really began as he held the kiss and lifted her off her feet, taking them both back to bed. She couldn't contain a giggle as he fumbled around, stripping the robe off her shoulders and shoving his boxers down and out of the sheets.

But the laughter soon died in her throat, the victim of her humming moans of pleasure. His clever fingers danced along her body while his mouth came down on the tight peak of a nipple—and she was a goner.

Entwining her legs with his, she got as close as she could but it was still not close enough. "Please, now," she said in a breathless voice she barely recognized. "We'll do all the other stuff—but later. Right now I need…"

"Elana, wake up, darlin'."

Gage's insistent demand irritated her. Before anything else happened, she wanted to go on with what they were…

"What?" Opening her eyes, she saw him hovering over her trying to untangle their bodies, and realized where she was. And who she was—Elana Kelly. "Oh, I was dreaming. But…" She clutched at his shoulders trying to hold him to her.

"It's time to get up," he mumbled as he tried backing away from her arms. "This—is not a good idea."

"Why not?" She wanted him so badly now she thought she might die of it.

"Because we'd both be thinking of someone else. This—" he waved a free hand between their bodies and tried scooting backward "—is just a matter of coincidence. It's not real."

"Wait." She nuzzled as close as he would let her and thrust her breasts against his chest.

What was so wrong with having one more blazing night to remember? Who would it hurt? "Let's just close our eyes. And we'll pretend to be whoever we want."

Chapter 6

Already as turned on as he'd been in years, Gage wondered why not? Why not spend a few hours pretending, if she was willing?

The lust he felt for her, this lush woman, was strong. Looking down into her eyes, he realized she was watching him with serious intent. Waiting for him to say something.

"I don't need to pretend," he said as he moved against her and pressed his erection into her belly. "But I didn't plan for this to happen. And I don't want you to feel like I'm taking advantage of the situation."

"It's me that's taking advantage, love." She kissed him again, wild and hungry. "And I didn't plan it, either."

Out of breath, he lifted his head. "Seriously, Elana. Be sure this is what you want. Another kiss like that one and it will be too late to stop. And I have nothing in mind beyond one night."

She gripped his shoulders and tugged him down to meet her lips. "Good," she whispered against him.

And then it was too late.

The next kiss was hot and amazing. Fiery and wet at the same time. He felt such a hunger in her, as though she'd been starving for his touch. It stoked his own needs, his own hunger, to a fevered pitch.

Leaning up on one elbow, he slowly unbuttoned her blouse and laid her open to his gaze. Her bra was white lace, more utilitarian than erotic, but he thought it was the sexiest thing he'd seen in longer than he could remember.

"Hold on." She sat up and removed the impediments to his touch, the shirt and bra, while he sat back and indulged himself in the sight of her exposed breasts.

What a beauty she was. Lush, full peaked breasts, with peach-colored nipples just begging to be fondled and adored. At the moment, he didn't want to consider that her breasts seemed fuller than the way he remembered Alicia's. This wasn't about Alicia anymore. He only wanted to fill his hands and eyes with the woman lying beneath him.

A masterpiece on canvas could never match her intensity and simmering looks.

She tugged at his shirt buttons. "Too many clothes between us, to my way of thinking. Take it off."

Screw the buttons. He reached down and jerked the hem up and over his head. "Yes, ma'am."

Five long, lonely years dissolved in a blaze of heat as he lowered his head and drew her nipple into his mouth. Elana arched her back, letting him splurge on the feast of her body. And feast he did. He consumed her; tasting, sucking, nibbling and fanning the flames between them. Her body was pure shimmering smoothness under his hands and mouth, and he wondered how he had survived for so long without.

Reaching for his zipper, she tugged on it and the look in her eyes turned hazy with desperation. "Please," she begged.

He covered her hand with his as together they slowly lowered his zipper. "I..." He hadn't come prepared for this.

Then he remembered something. Standing, he shucked his jeans and dug in the pocket for his wallet. Deep inside one of the wallet's inside slots he found a couple of ancient condoms. They might be out of date, but still better than nothing for a one-night stand.

For no matter what else this would be, or what tomorrow would bring, tonight was definitely a one-night stand.

He threw the condom on the nightstand and loomed over her. "Take the rest off. Now."

"Gage." A whisper of desire in the night.

She scrambled to lose the slacks and panties. After she'd lain down and gazed up at him with longing, he discovered he couldn't move. She was so beautiful that he felt consumed by her. Paralyzed, mind and body, with arousal.

"Please...please," she begged again.

Taking his hand, she brought it to her belly and then pushed lower. That was all the coaxing he needed. He knelt on the bed beside her, letting his fingers draw erotic circles around her belly button. Sliding his hand lower along her fine flesh, he dipped his head and replaced his hand with his tongue.

Her breath caught and she squirmed when his fingers moved lower, tunneling through the curls at the apex of her thighs. "Gage." Her raspy whisper spoke to her growing need.

With the tip of his finger, he found her hot, wet center and eased inside. So tight. So slick. He used his thumb to manipulate her engorged nub, and she went wild, thrashing and rotating against his hand.

For an instant, he thought of Alicia. But then Elana

moaned something that sounded like Gaelic words and the thought flew out of his hazy mind. She was close to an edge. Real close. He could tell by her low moans of pleasure. But he was losing his self-control at too great a pace to keep her there until she came. It had been far too long for him.

Growling out an inaudible cuss word, he reached for the foil packet and covered himself. Before she reacted, he parted her thighs with a knee, moved over her and drove into her waiting warmth.

He'd wanted to pace his need. But he lost it instead. Lost all sense of where he was and who he was with. Had he ever wanted Alicia this badly? He couldn't remember ever wanting anyone this much and surely not this fast.

Pounding into her, he couldn't make himself slow down. Not even when the fear of being too rough finally dawned on him. But from somewhere outside the mists of his own need, he knew she was meeting his hips stroke for stroke. Knew she'd wrapped her legs around his waist and was crying out with breathless abandon while he plunged to her very center.

Sweating and beyond rational thought, he felt only vaguely aware of her nails biting into his shoulders. But he remained hyper-aware of her calling out his name as her internal body convulsed around him.

He rammed into her one last time, riding the wave of a shared release so explosive and intense that the whole room shook with the force of it. Seeing fireworks behind his eyelids, he drew out every last sensation.

Collapsing on top of her, he listened to his thundering pulse and tried to calm his erratic breathing. Seconds later he rolled to one side, capturing her in his arms and bringing her along as he went.

But the moment he'd tucked her in close to his heart, Gage knew he'd just done something stupid. Stupid because he still didn't know who she was for sure but understood very well that she wouldn't be sticking around long enough for him to find out.

And danged if suddenly he didn't want to know her better. He wanted to know what made her happy and sad. Whether she liked horses and rainy weather or fast cars and sunshine. And most of all, which of a thousand places to touch on her body was the one that pleasured her the most. He wanted endless hours of this euphoric feeling. And lots more of what they'd found in each other's arms tonight.

He felt tormented by not knowing exactly who she was. No way could she be his dead wife. Alicia was never known to be cruel. Besides, he would've recognized her in bed even after all these years, wouldn't he? At several points during their lovemaking his thoughts turned to Alicia. But then in the next moment the woman beneath him seemed a complete stranger who'd gotten under his skin in less than twenty-four hours. Was it his own heart that had caused him to make up similarities?

The confusion was driving him insane. But he couldn't help himself. He wanted her. Whoever she was.

Elana snuggled close to his chest, close enough to feel his heartbeat against her cheek. What a mistake she'd just made. Making love to him again would end up being the death of her.

They'd always been very different people. He was a hard-working private investigator with a savior complex. And she, the daughter of gypsy criminals, was on the verge of an identity crisis. But the sex...the sex had always been spectacular. Tonight was no exception. She'd almost forgotten the kind of pleasure Gage could provide. Or rather, she'd managed to push it out of her mind. But now she'd had a big fat reminder that would forever leave her longing for his touch and dreaming of his kiss.

He scared her to death. The man was seriously into saving people. Besides the sex, she'd fallen in love with big, strong, protective Gage Chance who seemed so honest and straightforward. And now, even though he still didn't seem sure of her true identity, he would be trying to save her new persona from whatever danger lurked around the next corner.

Good way to get himself killed, the idiotic man. And she was an even bigger imbecile for getting into bed with him.

Keeping her eyes closed, she breathed in his scent. Spice and musk and something indefinable that was all Gage. As much as this night had been a bad idea, she couldn't manage to regret it. She would pay for it, maybe for the rest of her life, but she would never be sorry they'd made love one last time.

Still, she felt changed by making love to him again. And it seemed clear that nothing she said or did would make him leave her and save himself. So it was time for the truth. That might not save him, but she owed it to him.

He stirred and began stroking her back, murmuring words she couldn't understand but got the gist of anyway. Torn, she wanted what he wanted—badly. More of what they'd just shared. But maybe if she moved away from him now, pretended what they'd done wasn't something she wanted to repeat, he would back off and give her the time to get herself together before she told him everything. Ah hell, who was she kidding? She was a terrific liar, but she'd never be able to pull that off.

She *should* get up. Say something. Start giving him the complete truth. *Should. Should.* Not a chance.

He groaned in her ear and slanted a kiss across her lips that sizzled all the way down her spine. Reaching for him and finding him hard and ready, she lost her mind as white heat and rock-hard satin singed her fingers. Any resolve she might've had left was totally lost while the room combusted around them.

Later was her last coherent thought as she rubbed the tip of his erection against the spot on her body that ached for him the most. She would make things right—but much later.

Gage reached for Alicia in his sleep. But when all he found was empty space in the bed beside him, he came awake with a start.

What the hell?

Looking around the room, he realized where he was. Not Alicia. Not home. It all came back with a thud. Judging by the clock on the nightstand, it was 5:00 a.m. and he'd been making love to Elana for most of the night. And it had been a night like no other. But where was she now?

The artificial light filtering in through the window was partially blocked by a heavy snowfall. It was really coming down hard now. Where was she?

Sitting up and putting his feet on the carpeted floor, he spotted a light coming from under the bathroom door. The door was cracked open slightly, and if he held his breath he could hear a mumbled conversation going on.

He stood and quickly located his coat. Sure enough, his sat phone was missing.

He took his first real breath since coming awake and realizing Elana wasn't in bed. Who would she be calling at this hour? He hoped it was only her daughter, but somehow he doubted that. Whoever it was could be connected to the men after her.

Why didn't he know which it was? He was good enough to sleep with but not good enough for the truth?

Suddenly pissed as hell, at her and himself, he stormed to the bathroom door determined to shake the truth out of her and replace it with some sense. But when he got close, he found he could hear at least her half of the conversation. He didn't much like eavesdropping, but he hated being lied to even more. Hesitating with his hand on the doorknob, he listened.

"No, he doesn't know yet," she said in a voice that had not a trace of an accent. "Because. Because I didn't want to tell him unless I had to. Now, I guess I must. I can't sneak out without waking him. I have to say *something*."

He felt like someone had hit him upside the head with a two-by-four. It was Alicia's voice, and she was talking about *him*.

"Yes, yes. I know," she went on. "I'll find a way to disappear again after I explain who I am. He'll be angry when he hears the truth. That should give me the space I need to leave him behind."

It took Gage all of ten seconds to put two and two together. And when he did, the emotions flooding him ran the gamut from mad as hell, to pure relief at finding her alive, to hurt and humiliation. He froze where he was, unable to process all he felt.

"It'll be okay," she added in that same hushed phone voice. "You just be ready to come get me when I call. We still have the Russians and my father to worry about."

That did it. He bolted into the bathroom and found her, standing totally naked before the mirror. Her eyes went wide with shock when she spotted him.

Danged if the truth wasn't evident in those very eyes staring wildly at him. Eyes he'd thought he would never see again. *Hazel* eyes. Alicia's eyes.

"Gage...I..." She set the phone down and turned to him. "Let me explain."

"Yeah, so you can spin me another pack of lies? No thanks, Alicia. You've done quite enough of that already."

"There were reasons for the lies. And I've regretted them every day since the day I disappeared."

"Disappeared?" He laughed but the sound was hollow and full of hurt. "Is that what you call it? You died. I watched you slip under the bridge. Damn it. I *grieved* for you."

His chest hurt so badly he figured he must be having a heart attack. "Why, Alicia?" His voice cracked and came out in a hoarse whisper. "Just tell me why?"

"My name is not Alicia." The cry in her voice sobered him up fast.

Anger flashed, strong and mind-numbing through his clogged brain. "No more lies." Wanting to shake the truth out of her, he fisted his hands at his side. "It's time for explanations."

She turned and grabbed for a towel. "I'm so sorry, Gage." When she faced him again, holding the towel in front of her, her face was a mask of pain. Her bottom lip trembled and her eyes brimmed with water.

Fake tears? "Stop it," he ordered. "Just stop it. Do you have any idea what you put me through? Not a day has gone by for the past five years that I haven't thought of you and wondered if you'd felt any pain when you died. And you're sorry? It nearly destroyed me when I couldn't find you in the water. I have never felt so helpless.

"I want to know why you faked your death." He took a deep breath, trying to calm down. "Why you're living as someone else. And most of all, if you were in trouble, why didn't you let me help you? I thought we loved each other."

"You didn't know me." Before she turned away, he saw her face. No tears in sight.

Rage made him blind and desperate. Reeling, he took a step back but quickly recovered. Taking her by the shoulders, he gave her a hard shake. "Tell me."

"Everything I told you about my background when we

were married was a lie," she said with such a calm demeanor that it shook him even more. "But I want to tell you the truth now. You should know."

"You wouldn't know the truth if it came wrapped in a gold ribbon." He squeezed her arms, wanting to pry the story from her lips.

"You're hurting me." She raised her shoulders and tried to squirm away.

He loosened his grip but didn't let go. "Start with the name. Who are you?"

"I was born Amara Coppersmith. The daughter of American Rom parents. We're gypsies, Gage. Just like I said. *Everything* I said about my family...about the arranged marriage...that part was all true."

"Was I the guy in your story? The dumb one you used? Why did you find it necessary to fake your death? Did you hate me so much that you had to run away from me, too?"

She looked up at him, her face stricken with pain. "I could never hate you, Gage. That was just a story. And I'm truly sorry for the hurt I caused. Faking a drowning was stupid. But I didn't have a lot of time to make better plans. My father and the Russian mob boss had spotted me just that morning. The idea of drowning was Brendan's."

"Why didn't you tell me you were in trouble? Let me help?" He couldn't breathe. Could barely hear her voice anymore because of the drumbeat of his own pulse.

"Brendan was close by and knew the background. I needed to get out of town that day. He had the contacts to make it happen. You would never have let me go alone. I know you. You would've wanted to save me. I couldn't let you do that."

Something snapped inside him. "I didn't know you, but you knew everything about me?" He pushed her against the wall and got right in her face.

Her eyes widened again—until she looked down between them and saw a truth he couldn't hide. "I promise you, Gage," she said, reaching for him. "I didn't leave because I was unhappy. Not with you. You made my life wonderful for the very first time."

"You haven't answered the most important question," he snarled, dragging her lush body flush against him.

"Forgive me for the lies." Looping her arms around his neck, she went up on tiptoes and rubbed her breasts against his chest. "Are you asking about the sex? The sex between us was always the best. That hasn't changed if that's what you want to know."

He grabbed her bottom, lifted her up. "Put your legs around me."

She did what he asked, reaching between them to position him to her opening. "Yes, Gage. Yes, I want this, too."

Flexing his hips, he plunged into her. "Tell me," he demanded against her mouth.

He buried himself deep in her waiting heat. "Did you ever love me?" The question was nearly lost as he planted kisses along her jawline and squeezed her bottom to dive in even deeper.

Her head rolled and she started to moan. "Gage..."

"Answer me," he ground out as he held himself still. "Did you *ever* really love me? Or was it all a lie?"

"Please." She rocked her hips against his. "Now."

This wasn't just about sex for him. It was about healing. And about love. And most of all about possession.

"Did. You. Love. Me?"

"I loved you," she gasped. "Oh, God, how I loved you."

His mind went blank. He began pumping into her, catching her screams in his mouth and relishing every second. When she squeezed her thighs together, the earth stood on its head.

Her orgasm was so powerful it took him right along for the craziest ride of his life. Moments later as she continued convulsing around him, he felt his knees buckle.

Still breathing heavily, he lowered her feet so she could reach the floor. But he left his hands on her hips to keep them both steady. Leaning his forehead against the wall, he felt utterly destroyed.

A few seconds later, she stirred and lightly pushed on his chest. "Now we both need a shower."

He moved aside but hung on to a towel bar for balance.

"I want you to know," she began as she turned on the water. "I still love you. More than ever."

He reached for her again, ready for a repeat performance.

She held him at arm's length. "But I must tell you the whole truth. I can't live with the lies between us. I'll be out in a moment. Just wait."

Feeling like a complete imbecile, he said, "I'll be here. But nothing says I'll believe a thing you have to say."

Chapter 7

Elana had never faced anything this difficult. As she turned away from Gage and stepped into the shower, the look on his face, that combination of longing and regret, cost her something. It ripped a large chunk of her heart out and stomped it into dust.

Dear Lord, she felt dirty. But no amount of washing would take away the stains of her betrayal. She was so ashamed of the way she'd used him—not only during the night for sex, but also for their entire relationship. He and his isolated ranching community in west Texas had made wonderful ports in the storm—for a while. But she'd married him knowing full well that it wouldn't last. It couldn't. They were too different.

So, she'd begun by lying to him. And she planned on one more lie. However, this one would be a lie by omission. If she told him everything...

No, that wasn't an option.

She was surprised he hadn't asked the moment he realized who she was. But there hadn't been time. Not yet. He was probably still in shock. Maybe if she dressed and told him most of the story in a hurry, she could hold off on the inevitable.

Listening to him run water in the sink, she quickly ducked under the shower, soaped up and rinsed off. Ten minutes later she got out to dry off and he'd already left the bathroom.

With no choice but to go into the next room dressed only in one large, fluffy towel around her middle, she grabbed a hand towel for her hair, lifted her chin and prayed for a miracle reprieve. When she opened the bedroom door, she found him fully dressed and looking out the window with his back to her.

"Are you willing to listen?" she asked, hoping he had calmed down.

"I'll listen. But how will I know what you're saying isn't another lie?"

She couldn't do this while naked, so she scavenged around inside her duffel for underwear, heavy jeans and a sweater. "You'll know because as much as you don't know *who* I am, you do know *me*. The me inside. Let your heart decide what's the truth."

He turned and folded his arms across his chest. "Go on."

After dressing and pulling the sweater over her head, she found her knees were shaking too badly to keep standing. With the hand towel still wrapped around her hair, she made her way to the table and sat in one of the chairs. Gage remained standing, looming above her.

"I'll begin by saying that my heritage *is* American Rom—gypsy." She waited for his look of disgust, but it didn't come. "But for some reason I was always the smart child. So smart that when my teachers begged my father to let me continue schooling past the time most young Roma girls quit, he gave in and let me go on. Little girls in our community are usually destined to be housewives—the heads of the household. But my father loves me very much and somehow knew I needed to be different."

"Your father... Does he know where you are?" Gage took a step toward her.

"No. At least, I don't think he does. But these men—they may be part of the same Russian mob." Folding her arms around her waist to keep herself steady, she went on. "As my high school graduation approached, the talk turned to college. But no one in my family ever went to college before. Still, my father could see it would be best for me. Unfortunately, the family couldn't afford school. And we're not the kind who would borrow money."

"Not even for..."

"Never. That's just the way it is with us." She sighed and looked away, not able to watch Gage's stern, unbelieving expression. "Something happened around that time. A Russian Rom family immigrated to our town. One of their sons was about my age. My mother and his mother decided to arrange our marriage like all Roma elders do for their children."

"So that part wasn't a lie?" Gage took the seat across from her.

"All true, I'm afraid." She felt her body caving in on itself as she came to the ugly part of the story. "But what I didn't mention was that this Russian family was heavily into criminal activities and had become wealthy. It seems they'd been involved with the Russian mob back in their homeland. And yet, they still expected a dowry from our family."

She let the sad smile spread across her face but went on. "We had nothing. Less than nothing. I didn't want the marriage, anyway. But my father went to the boy's father and struck a deal. Our family would work for their family, doing whatever they wanted us to do, until we could pay off the dowry."

"Becoming criminals? Your father sold his soul so you could be married to a guy you hardly knew?"

"He also promised to pay for a couple of years of college for me, but yeah, that's the way it was. Nice story, right? It's one of the reasons I seldom think about my past. And I've never talked about it to anyone before."

"But your friend Brendan, the one from the store and the one who has your child, he knows?"

"He knows. He's a distant relative on my mother's side and isn't involved in any criminal activity. I went to him for help because I knew he had connections and wouldn't tell my parents."

"So who is it that's after you?"

Without answering him directly, she whimpered, "This is all my fault. I shouldn't have wanted an education so badly. My mother thought marrying into wealth would ensure my happiness. Instead, I've ruined our whole family."

"Who has been shooting at us?" His eyes narrowed on her.

He was right. He deserved an answer before they parted ways. "I would imagine it's the Russian Roma mob—in addition to my ex-fiancé, or my own father and his brothers."

"Let me get this straight. You claim your old *fiancé*…" The way he drew out that word pained her, the same as if he'd stabbed her with a knife. "…and your father are after you. Why? Why after all this time would your father want to kill you?"

Drying her hair with the towel, she knew it was nearing time for her to leave. "It probably isn't my father's doing. He would never want to see me hurt. But his mob boss may be making him go along. You have to understand…"

Dragging in air, she raced ahead. "In the gypsy culture,

especially with the Russians, you can never go back on a deal. Anyone who does has to be taught a lesson."

"You sure it isn't anything else?" His voice had grown even darker, if that was possible.

Standing, she finished her hair with the towel as best she could and slipped into her shoes. "What do you mean?"

"You didn't steal anything from them, did you?"

Oh, man, where was he going with this? "No, of course not. I may be related to criminals, but I'm not into petty theft."

Scrunching up his mouth in a frown, he tilted his head. "So all this time, even while we were a couple, you knew they would be coming after you eventually." Not a question.

She answered him, anyway. "Yes, I suppose that's right. But I thought we were safe at your ranch. I thought…"

"And you didn't bother to tell me?" He interrupted her with a snarl. "Didn't think I was important enough to know about the danger?"

Oh, Gage. "I didn't want you to worry. I thought I'd lost them while we were living at the Chance ranch. But then that day in Austin—they spotted me. Finally figured out where I was. I knew I would have to run again."

"Still without telling me. Was I in danger?"

She shook her head with as much force as humanly possible. "No. Never. But I knew you soon would be if we stayed together. They're too strong. You can't beat them. All you can do is run, and I knew you would never accept that."

Picking up her discarded clothes from last night, she stuffed them in her bag and reached for her coat. She had to get out of this room *now*.

Just as she reached for the door handle he came toward her. "You're leaving without finishing our conversation? Without saying goodbye? I should've known."

With the door already open, she turned back but had to

fight off the tears. "I'm sorry, Gage. It has to be this way. I've been trying to tell you. We can't stay together. I need to leave."

"And you don't want me to come? To help?"

"You can't. You'll die if you try. There's too many of them. You need to leave town this morning. Quickly. Quietly. Or you might as well let them kill me now because if they hurt you, it will kill me, anyway. I do love you. I never lied about that."

He heaved a heavy sigh and stepped back. "So, you've done all this—faked your death, gone into hiding and lied about everything just to keep me safe?"

"I haven't lied about everything." Now her voice was cracking and her heart felt like someone hit it with a sledgehammer. "I did lie about some things. But it *was* to keep you safe. And I do love you."

He took another step in her direction and she panicked. "But I don't want you around." Her voice rose as she fought to find a way to keep him alive. "I can handle this alone, don't you understand? Forget about me. Go home. But be careful about leaving. And when you get back to Texas, go on with your life. I don't ever want to see you again."

She dashed through the door in such pain it left her running doubled-over. How was she ever supposed to survive this?

Only two things kept her moving. Kept her flying down the stairs. Gage would be safe—and alive. And she would stay alive, too—for their daughter.

No, dang it. Gage grabbed his gear and went out the door after her. She was not leaving him behind before she answered *all* his questions. And they hadn't even touched on the most important one.

Since he'd seen her last, she'd had a child. And she'd

given birth to that child within twelve months after her faked death.

He was fairly sure the little girl could not be his daughter. Even as much as she'd lied, that was one thing Alicia would've told him. Or he would've just known that she'd been pregnant when they were together. He *knew* who she was inside. She'd been right about that. So that meant there had to be some other man in her life within weeks of her leaving. Someone she'd run to when she ran away from him.

That knowledge hurt. Hurt badly, because the two of them had talked about having kids someday. He'd been all for it but she'd wanted to wait.

Since the moment this morning when he'd first been sure of her identity, he'd wanted to ask the question. He'd hesitated then because he was afraid of the answer. And later because he'd been so shaken, and because he'd had his hands full—of her.

But she couldn't just announce that she still loved him and not give him a chance to get all his questions answered. She couldn't just tell him that she'd left him behind to protect him. That was bull. Apparently she excelled at lying. But he had already made up his mind that one fact, at least, would be answered truthfully before this was over.

He saw her darting away from the bottom of the open stairwell and chased down the stairs to catch up. Despite what she'd said, what she thought, he could do a better job at protection than she would do on her own. They'd beat the threat together.

And then she would give him the truth about the child's father before it was his turn to walk away from her—for good.

After entering the lobby at the bottom of the stairs, he couldn't find her. He gave the large open space a thorough looking-over and finally spotted her, inching along the wall toward the front desk and a bank of phones. She must be trying to make a call without being seen.

Well, not if he reached her first.

Time had gotten away from him somehow this morning. Almost 8:00 a.m. Already? People were sitting in the lobby, drinking coffee from a bar and waiting for the restaurant to open. Most of the boutique shops were beginning to open their doors, too, hoping the tourists would want to do some last-minute Christmas shopping before heading to the slopes.

Too many people and too much commotion. He couldn't tell where the threat would be coming from.

Acting casual, Gage wound through the lounge area. About midway to the front desk, he came across a man reading a newspaper who seemed out of place. With his hair in a ponytail, a diamond stud winking from one ear and a wireless phone receiver attached to the other, the guy could've easily passed as one of the other holiday skiers. But this one wasn't dressed in ski attire. Or in after-ski attire, for that matter. The heavy-set man wore a dark suit, white shirt and tie.

No question. He did not belong in this picture.

Gage picked up his pace. By the time he reached the front desk, Elana was on the phone and Ponytail Guy was getting to his feet and speaking a mile a minute into his earpiece. Uh-oh.

Snagging her elbow with one hand, Gage ripped the phone away from her with the other and then slammed the receiver back in its cradle. "Time to go. Your past has caught up to you."

Elana jerked back and glared up at him. "What do you...?" The words died in her mouth when he nodded his head toward the man in a dark suit who by now was headed their way.

Fighting her own agitation, Elana sized up the situation in an instant and quickly realized the parking area and front door lay on the other side of the Russian coming toward them.

Now there was no choice but to help Gage find a way out of here. It was too late to split up again. Like it or not, they were in this together.

She remembered Gage's trick from yesterday of leaving through the restaurant's back entrance. But this restaurant's doors weren't open yet. That way would be a dead end.

Just then the glass doors to the high-end jewelry and gift shop opened and she saw their route to salvation. "Come on," she whispered as she grabbed his arm. "This way."

Hanging on to him with a death grip, she barged into a crowd and dodged her way past a dozen people lining up for breakfast. "Sorry," she mumbled as she plowed right into the back of a woman and knocked her off balance.

Gage said nothing but managed to keep up with her antics. "Where the devil are we headed?" he finally growled as they cleared the bulk of the crowd.

"Here." She raced into the tight space of the gift store and sought out the man heading behind a counter. "Earl, can you help us out?"

"Well, morning, Elana. What can I do for you?"

Gasping for a breath, she answered on a wispy thread. "I can't explain right now, but we need a way out of here without being seen. Is there an employee entrance?"

"Someone after you?" Earl's million-dollar smile reminded her of what a jokester he was.

"Sort of. But we didn't do anything wrong." She gritted her teeth and tried to remain calm. "Please, Earl. I'll tell you all about it later. I promise."

Something in the tone of her voice must've convinced him that this was an emergency because he moved to the front door, shut it and locked it with the keys still in his hand. "I'll show you. This way."

Three minutes later he unlocked the back door to the hotel and let them outside into a delivery zone. "You owe me answers, Elana." Earl muttered his goodbyes as they stepped out into one of the worst snowstorms she could remember.

"Join the crowd, buddy," Gage grumbled, shaking his hand.

The next thing she knew, Gage had her arm again and they were sliding at breakneck speed over icy asphalt toward the guest parking. Her brain was racing, too, trying to figure out a way for them to escape. Where to go?

It looked like wherever they went, they were going together. Not the smartest move, but it seemed their only choice from this point.

Gage dug into his jeans pocket and pulled out the rental keys. "Glad we didn't valet last night. Get in."

Climbing into the passenger seat and throwing her duffel into the back, she'd barely closed the door when he roared off. "Do you know where you're going?"

"Down the mountain," he ground out. "Away from this storm and those goons. We'll head back toward L.A. and the airport."

It hit her then. "We can't. There's only one road down. It's a four-lane highway, but they can easily stake it out and lie in wait for us."

"We can't stay in Piñon Lake. There's no place left to hide." They'd reached the edge of the resort property and he had to make a left or a right.

"Go left. The road narrows about a mile up there, but it winds through the mountains and eventually goes back to civilization the long way around."

"You're out of your mind." He gestured toward the windshield. "Look out the window. It's snowing. A flipping blizzard. We'll be stuck before we get five miles out of town."

"Maybe someone will be plowing." She was grasping for an answer but figured anything was better than staying here much longer. "Brendan and his brothers own a cabin up there, just in case we need it. I've been there before."

Gage glanced into his rearview mirror. "I think we're about to have company." Turning left, he eased on the gas and struggled to keep the tires on the road.

He straightened out the car and turned on the windshield wipers for all the good they would do. "I sure hope you know how to pray. 'Cause, smart or not, here we go. Hang on."

Chapter 8

The headlights following behind them grew dimmer in the blinding snow. But after fifteen minutes of carefully negotiating the two-lane road, Gage knew the "good" part of their journey was almost over.

"I'm positive the highway patrol will be closing this road soon," he said without turning his eyes toward Elana. "We haven't seen many vehicles coming down past us since we left the hotel. In fact the only other cars on the road seem to be state troopers going up the mountain, probably to close the roads. Got any other ideas?"

"Just a few more miles and we'll turn off toward the cabin." Elana sat as still as a mouse.

"And what will *that* road look like?"

She shook her head. "I've only been there once before. I can't really remember, but I'm guessing it must be pretty decent 'cause the cabin's rented out during the winter sometimes. I do know it's only one lane, though."

"Terrific." He stopped talking to concentrate on his driving.

Then the tires slipped and the nose of the SUV headed toward the edge of what he figured would be a deep canyon. Fighting his impulse to swing the wheel the other way, he turned into the skid until the tires caught again.

Whew. That was close. He refused to think about how far down that canyon floor might be. But he was pretty sure those were the tops of evergreens he'd been seeing as they'd driven close to the edge. And judging by the trees on the other side of the road, they could reach heights of eighty to a hundred feet.

Checking his rear mirror, he spotted headlights rounding the curve he'd just made. Before he could say anything about it, those lights disappeared once again and all he could see behind them was a blur of white. He sure hoped that was the state troopers again. Otherwise they were definitely in a world of trouble.

He should've known better than to let Elana talk him into going up the mountain instead of down. The road would be closed at any moment.

"The turnoff to the cabin should be right up ahead." Elana leaned forward, straining against the seat belt, in order to see out the windshield.

He slowed to a crawl, praying whoever followed behind would notice he'd slowed and not run right over the top of the SUV.

"Oh, there's a sign." Elana pointed toward the side of the road.

"Who can read that in this messy weather?"

"Well, not me. But I remember seeing a road signpost a few feet from the turnoff. There. Turn here!"

If the tires would grab traction, he'd be happy to turn. Holding his breath, he eased the vehicle to the right, hoping to hell a cabin in the mountains could be their ticket out of this trouble.

The road suddenly narrowed down to what he'd call a lane while giant pines growing along both sides made it feel like they were driving through a tunnel. "You know, we don't get weather like this very often in west Texas." And he wished to hell he knew how to negotiate it better.

"We don't get anything this bad up here very often, either," she told him with a hollow voice. "Most years the ski slopes have to resort to making snow. I'd guess this must be the storm of the decade."

"Figures," he grumbled.

Dark as pitch, he couldn't be sure where the road went. His headlights only illuminated about ten feet ahead. So at a snail's pace, they crawled along inch by inch.

"How are we going to know when we get there?" Elana's tense voice crawled down his spine and gave him the chills.

"Let's hope the road ends at the cabin and doesn't lead on into a lake or over a cliff." Now why did he have to say that?

"Yeah," she agreed in a shaky whisper.

"Look, it'll be okay." He needed to say something to calm her. "I haven't seen any headlights behind us since we turned off the mountain road. That's one good thing. And we'll find the cabin. If it's on this lane, we'll find it."

"If?" Elana began fidgeting in her seat. "What if I was wrong and this isn't the right way?"

"Easy there. We'll be okay. If nothing else…" The beam of his headlights lit up a mailbox a few feet away. "Is this it?"

The breath whooshed out of her lungs. "Oh, thank God. Yes. This is it. Pull up the driveway next to that mailbox and park close to the front door."

Gage couldn't imagine who would deliver mail to this godforsaken out-of-the-way place. Civilized Texans placed their mailboxes on the nearest main highway. Or they picked up their mail in town.

But he was relieved to think that in a few more minutes they would be out of the weather. "Okay, we're here," he said as he parked and looked through the windshield at what he could see of the cabin.

"The key should be under the pot next to the front door."

"That's imaginative. You ready? I'll leave the headlights on until we're inside."

Without answering, she took a big breath of air, unbuckled and opened the door.

Gage turned off the engine and just sat there watching her at the front door, wondering how the holy hell he had ever gone so far down this rabbit hole. So far, in fact, that he might never be able to climb back out.

Andrei Krayev stepped up into the driver's seat of the four-wheel drive rental pickup truck, glad to be out of the storm and worried about facing his father with this news. "The state trooper says the road is closed. We must go back."

"Have they seen any sign of the man and that woman?" Dimitri Krayev sat sweating in front of the hot air blasting from the truck's heater.

"No. They claim no one has come this way."

"And?" He narrowed his eyes and Andrei felt the scorn down to his toes.

"I asked, Father. The authorities said perhaps the other vehicle turned off before coming this far. Apparently there are several cabins located along this route but they're situated off the road in deep woods."

"Is it possible their vehicle went over the side in the storm?"

Andrei didn't like thinking about that. As much as Amara

Coppersmith had treated him like a piece of garbage stuck to the bottom of her shoe, he still wouldn't want to see her die.

At least not quickly.

"If their vehicle went over the side, the authorities won't begin a search until the weather clears." He thought back to the winters of his youth in the Ukraine. "They might not be found until the spring thaw." People, dead bodies, were lost in snowdrifts for months, sometimes for years.

"We will go back and search each cabin until I am satisfied," Dimitri announced.

Andrei didn't mind the extra work. He was every bit as eager to locate the traitorous woman as his father.

He backed up the pickup and began to turn around just as the state trooper had directed. "We'll find them, Father. Ivan and his men will be joining us any minute. With so many looking, it shouldn't take too long to locate one foolish couple."

Chapter 9

Elana banged through the cabin's door, hardly noticing the cold or her frozen fingers. But after turning on a light and glancing around, the frosty look of everything inside reminded her how numb she felt. Two minutes later she found the propane generator switch out back and flipped on the heat. It would take a few minutes but at least they'd be warm soon.

"This is cozy." With his arms full of their bags, Gage plowed into the room as he kicked the front door shut with his foot.

"It will be. Shouldn't take long to warm up." But in the meantime, she wasn't going to sit anywhere.

He didn't seem inclined to rest his bottom on any of the ice-cold looking furniture, either. After he dropped the bags near the door, he paced the front room while clapping his hands together to stay warm.

She had a better idea of how to keep warm. Body temperature. It was all she could do not to step into his arms and beg him to hold her close. But that was probably a thing of the past. Their time as lovers was over.

Still, visions of making love to him while she whispered all her secrets and told him again how much she loved him crept into her numb mind and began to warm her thoughts. An intimate and compelling image, it made her pulse pound and her mouth water with wanting.

She knew better. Knew that Gage was too wounded at this point to give her an inch. In fact, he might never come around. Might always hate her. Hate was the opposite side of love, and right now Gage balanced on the edge.

All that they'd ever meant to each other had been destroyed or soon would be. And she'd been the one to murder those feelings.

Since that scary ride up the mountain, she'd come to the conclusion that it was time to give up the whole story. Soon. Tonight. Because she had an overwhelming feeling they might not live to see tomorrow.

"There must be a better way to warm up." Gage opened the first door he came to and turned on the light. "The kitchen. Do you think there's coffee?"

"I'm sure there is. Shall I make us some?"

He disappeared into the kitchen but called out an answer. "I'll do it. Give me a moment."

She'd almost forgotten that Gage had been the cook in the family. Her childhood hadn't exactly consisted of cooking lessons. Everyone in her family worked in the family business.

When she peeked into the kitchen, he'd already found the coffee and started the coffeemaker. "Smells good. Can we find something to cook so we can turn on the stove or the oven? It's still freezing in here."

"Hot coffee will help." He reached for a couple of mugs.

"But yeah, we can preheat the oven, too. Not sure what we'll find to eat, though."

"Brendan's brothers always keep the place stocked. They use it themselves as a retreat and sometimes they rent it out."

"Are you hungry?" He poured the coffee and handed her a steaming mug.

"Not at all." Her stomach rolled when she thought of what lay ahead.

Once she'd managed to pass a couple of sips of the searing hot, black liquid past her lips and tongue, she felt stronger. "We need to figure out where to go from here."

Without removing her coat, she sat at the small kitchen table, waiting while Gage turned on the oven. "I think we're probably safe here while the storm rages," she told him. "No one in their right mind would stay out in weather like this for long. Not even a dangerous Russian mob. But it could quit snowing at any moment. We need a plan."

"I agree. Hold that thought." He reached deep into his coat pocket. "Let me try the sat phone, see if I can get a signal."

Would it really be as easy as just calling for help?

Staring at the phone in his hand, Gage shook his head. "Low battery. But all it will take is a few minutes plugged in and we'll get through." He found the cord and a wall plug.

"Who can you call?"

"The cops in L.A.," he said while checking the power. "Or maybe I should try contacting my friend at the L.A. FBI office. He'd know best what law enforcement agency to call in. I'm afraid the Piñon Lake community has a small force and they'll have their hands full with weather-related problems."

"You're right. The town has only one sheriff and two deputies. They'd be no match for the Russian mob. But L.A.'s at least three hours away. Shouldn't we plan an escape just in case?"

Gage pulled out the other chair at the table, turned it around and straddled it. "If we had a good way out of here without being seen, we'd be taking it right now. Just stay calm. We'll let the authorities come to the rescue. We should've called them in the first place."

"And that's my fault," she groaned. "Like everything else. Why'd you have to follow me? I tried to tell you that separately we'd have a better chance."

"I disagree. If I hadn't followed, you might already be in the Russians' hands. Or dead."

Elana lowered her forehead to the table and heaved a heavy sigh. She wasn't sure she could look at him for the next few minutes.

"I'm...*fairly* sure they won't kill me," she told him quietly. "If they're like other gypsies, they just want their property back."

"But you don't know that for a fact." Gage sounded frustrated. "And they've already been shooting at you. I'd say that means they don't care much what kind of shape you're in when they bring you home."

"You may be right. But what I do know for a fact is now that they've taken notice of *you,* they will want to see you dead. Interference in gypsy business is not taken lightly."

Gage remained silent for such a long time that she raised her head to study him.

"So, we're back to the excuse that you have done all this..." He waved a hand between them. "Leaving me in Texas, changing your name and looks and then trying to leave me behind here, all in order to keep me safe?" He drew himself up in the chair and stared her down. "I don't buy it. You know I can take care of myself. And I would've taken better care of you, too, if only I'd known what you were up against. But you chose to shut me out."

"Gage, please. Can't you just believe I'm telling the truth this one time? There are too many of them. And I was always sure you'd receive much harsher treatment from the Russians than I would. Really. I didn't—don't—want to see you hurt."

He scraped his chair around and stood, looming over her. "I—" Cutting off his own words, he seemed to change his mind. "Hold it. It's been long enough. Let me try the phone again."

Picking it up, he dialed. "Got through," he mumbled almost to himself.

While Gage talked to his FBI pal, Elana rummaged in the cabinets looking for something to eat that would be quick and easy. She still wasn't hungry, but she figured they'd need sustenance if they were to fend off an attack by the Russians.

And she was sure an attack was imminent.

She found crackers, a can of tuna and a can of peaches. Not exactly breakfast food, but she'd have it on the table in moments.

By the time Gage clicked off his call and returned to the table, she'd set it with small plates and silverware. He barely seemed to notice.

"We should have help very soon," he told her. "The FBI will marshal forces from both the L.A. and state police to come to our aid. My buddy checked with the weatherman and he says this storm is just about to blow over. The cops are readying a couple of their helicopters and they've already contacted the state patrol."

He put away the phone and came toward the table. "From my description and from what you told me, the FBI is quite anxious to talk to these particular Russians. Seems they've been looking for a lead to them for a long time. The minute the weather breaks our rescuers will be on the way."

"I hope they're in time." She'd said the optimistic words, but deep down she doubted that the two of them would still be here and in one piece by the time their rescuers arrived. "Sit and eat something. I want to finish our conversation before...help arrives."

Pulling back the chair, he sat at the table with her. He picked up his fork and dug in to the peaches without a word.

"I need to...say something," she began with a slight hesitation in her voice and in her mind. "But first, please believe that I love you, Gage. I have always loved you and I'll never love anyone the same way. I suspect you no longer love me, and I deserve that. But you must believe me..."

Her voice failed and she had to sniff back a tear.

Before she could finish her sentence, he jumped in. "If you've always been so much in love with me, how come you found someone else so soon after you left?"

"What?" She'd absently picked up a cracker, but at that remark, she dropped it back to the plate as the blood rushed from her head. "I don't understand. What are you saying? There's never been anyone else."

He stood and glared at her. "Bull. You couldn't have been out of my sight for more than a few days when you fell into bed with someone else. Was it that Russian fiancé of yours? Is that why his father and your father are so determined to find you?"

Stunned, she felt like someone had pushed her off a cliff. She couldn't catch her breath.

"Come on, Alicia or Elana or whoever you are, admit it. That's the real reason they're chasing you. You took his daughter, their grandchild, with you when you disappeared."

A laugh erupted from her throat before she could call it back. But to her ears, the tone of that laugh sounded a lot more hysterical than amused. He couldn't possibly believe what he'd just said.

A second glance at his hard-set mouth and narrowed eyes told her that he had indeed believed every word of the tale he'd just spun. She'd wondered why he hadn't asked about her child yet. This was the reason. His mind had created a scenario that seemed more plausible than any other.

She started for him, wanting to soothe, to cradle him in her arms and make him understand. But he backed away from her touch.

He must really hate her, but he deserved the truth, no matter what happened after that. "Gage, my darling. Gay, the daughter I named after you, is your child. When I left, I had no idea I was pregnant. She was born almost nine months exactly from our last week together. There wasn't anyone else. Not ever. You are her father."

For a second she thought he hadn't heard, but then his face turned as pale as hers had felt only moments before. "No. I don't believe that."

"It's true. If it's important to you, and if we make it out of here alive, feel free to have DNA tests done."

Once again she took a step in his direction. She needed to touch him, to feel his warmth. But the look in his eyes was cold as ice.

"I want to meet her," he growled, and the tone of his voice forced her backward.

"Of course you can. She's a wonderful little girl. A bit on the independent side, but I suspect she gets that from you."

"How could you do this?" He groaned and turned his back to her. "How could you not tell me before? That's... that's... I don't know you at all. I guess I never really knew you."

Elana wanted to die. The hatred in his words bit into her heart like a whip.

Her whole body shook. Her pulse pounded as though she'd run a mile. This was much worse than she'd ever imagined.

She tried to control her thoughts, her voice. What if one or both of them lived through this day somehow?

"Gage," she began tentatively. "You need a way to reach her in case I don't make it and you do. That phone call I made last night on your phone to Brendan—he and his wife have her. You'll be able to find her by contacting him. They're in hiding, but use that number."

"Oh, don't worry. I'll find her. Whether you make it or not. If she's my daughter, she'll be going home with me."

Feeling as though he were squeezing her by the throat, Elana ran to him and grabbed him by the arm. "You can't mean you'd take her away from me. You couldn't be that cruel."

He swung around to face her and tore his arm from her grip. "So, you can keep my daughter from me, but I don't get the same privilege? Wanna bet? You are not exactly a stable mother, you know. No judge would ever let you keep her after everything you've done."

"But…" Her legs gave out from under her and she sank to her knees. "Couldn't we share her time? Make some arrangement like that?"

It was his turn to laugh as he stood over her, but then again, the sound was hollow. "I'm not even sure there is a child at this point. I don't believe a word you've ever told me. And to insist you've done all this in the name of loving me is beyond ridiculous. You're on your own from here out. After the storm is over, I intend to get to the truth. Without any interference from you."

He narrowed his eyes and fisted his hands. "Stay away from me."

She wondered if somehow she'd missed him physically

reaching inside her body and ripping out her heart while it was still beating. Her chest couldn't hurt any more if he had. But somehow she managed to get to her feet and stumble to the front door.

He followed her. "Where do you think you're going?"

"Do you care?" She intended to go to the main highway and try to find the Russians before they could get to him.

He was right. She was a terrible person. A chronic liar and a cheat. Her whole existence had been worthless. The one right thing she could still do in her life would be to protect him from harm. She could make a deal with the Russians and give herself up. Her father probably wouldn't actually let them kill her. She could just go away with them, and both Gage and Gay would be safe. She hoped.

Gage reached up and slammed his hand against the front door so she couldn't open it. "Don't be a fool."

"I'm staying away from you like you said."

"There's a snowstorm out there, and the gunmen chasing us could show up any moment. Wait for the cops."

"You wait." *Please.* "I'll find the Russians and tell them you dropped me off and are long gone by now. They won't kill me." *Probably.*

He took his arm away to reach for her shoulder, but she already had her hand on the doorknob. She twisted it and her body faster than he moved and was outside in a blink.

"Dang it, woman. Don't be…"

The words died in his throat as he opened the door wide right behind her. Not only had it stopped snowing and the skies were clearing, but right then three big, black pickups pulled into the yard.

Oh, man, they'd been found already. Now what the devil would they have to do to survive?

Chapter 10

Gage didn't waste any time and took no arguments. He grabbed Elana by the arm and dragged her back into the house before anyone could step out of the trucks.

"There's a rear door to this place, right?" Never stopping, he swung his case up on the way through the living room and dug out his Glock.

Not that it would be of any use at a distance. But if—or when—things got more intense, he didn't want to face the bad guys unarmed.

"Gage, wait." Elana hung back.

"Not a chance. Get moving."

As he unlocked the back door and stuck his head out to make sure no one was waiting, she said, "Let me talk to them. I'll say you ran away. They should be happy just to get me back. Maybe they'll forget about you."

"That's doubtful. They must've spotted me a moment ago, and I'll bet they don't want any loose ends. Besides, what are you planning on doing with your life if they do take you alive? Who would take care of your daughter? Or would you force her into the same life you had?"

"*Our* daughter. And I wanted you to raise her. That's one of the reasons why it's so important for you to live through this."

He pulled her through the door and out into the cold. Moving quickly toward a stand of trees about thirty feet away, he growled at her over his shoulder. "One of the reasons?"

Tugging mightily against him, she tried digging in her heels but they slipped against the snow. "*I love you,* damn it. You must stay safe."

He almost rolled his eyes, but there wasn't time to call her a liar again. "Come on!"

They'd nearly reached the cover of the forest when a shot rang out. He hadn't grown up on a Texas ranch for nothing. That was the sound of a rifle. They were outgunned.

Dropping her arm, he turned and raised his hands to his head. "Pretend we're giving up. I need them to come closer. I want them in range."

"This isn't going to work," she whispered as she, too, turned. "If they get close enough, you're a dead man."

"We'll see."

"Gage, I can't let you…"

"Well, well, Amara, have you finally stopped running?" One gunman with a rifle, a young man of about thirty, stepped from around the corner of the cabin and drew a bead on her head.

"Hello, Andrei." She didn't answer his question but tried to edge ahead of where Gage stood.

Gage thought about her move for a moment and decided to let her temporarily cover him while he reached for the Glock he'd stuck in the waistband of his jeans.

"You don't look like a ghost to me." The fellow with the rifle stopped aiming at any particular target as his rifle tip lifted. "How is it that you've come back from the dead?"

"Ah, Andrei, you are still quite the joker. Is my father with you?"

Andrei didn't have a chance to answer because right then an older man, one that clearly looked in charge, came around the cabin's corner. Instead of a rifle, this man was armed with a .38 semiautomatic. Was this her father? Or the Russian mob boss?

Gage felt he'd be fast enough to take both men if he could find some kind of distraction. But he worried about where the rest of the men who'd arrived in those black pickups were right now. And how many men exactly was he dealing with here?

"Your father won't be joining us," the older man said with a heavy Russian accent. He took a couple of steps closer but kept the barrel of his weapon pointed at the ground.

"Hello, Dimitri," Elana said quietly. "I'm flattered that you consider me worthy of your time."

The old man flicked the tip of his gun in a dismissive gesture. "I am here accompanying my son. He believes a promise was made that must be honored in a way that will satisfy him. I am not so forgiving."

Elana inched fully in front of Gage, blocking most of his body from the Russians' view. He noticed her trembling and could feel her fear as he drew closer to her side.

"Are you willing to trade?" Elana's voice sounded much stronger than he knew she felt. "I demand that you satisfy the Roma honor creed. Listen to my terms."

Both Russian men remained silent but didn't drop their weapons.

"I will trade myself for the life of this outsider. He means nothing to—"

Young Andrei broke in. "You have the nerve to talk of *honor?* And to dare offer such a trade? This—disgusting—outsider has broken the ritual purity laws. You are permanently tainted by his touch."

Andrei shifted his rifle and took a step closer. "I'll give you the gift of not killing you where you stand. Yet perhaps you would consider that preferable to what is to happen. You will come back with me—not as my wife as planned—but as my property. There will be many, many years for you to consider your treachery and to regret what you have done."

Elana turned her head toward Dimitri. "Where is my father? He won't stand for this kind of treatment."

Dimitri took a breath and silently raised his weapon.

Gage could wait no longer. As a shot rang out and whizzed by him, he grabbed Elana by the shoulder and pulled her behind him. Then, taking a quick shooter's stance, he fired at Dimitri before the older man could get off his next shot. A bloom of red blood blossomed on Dimitri's chest, and without saying a thing, he slowly sank to his knees.

"You killed my father!" Andrei screamed and aimed his rifle.

Gage suddenly lost his balance as Elana pushed him aside and stepped directly in front of him to block the shot. The two blasts coming from Andrei's rifle were not as far off the mark as his father's shot had been. Trying to regain his stance and reach her at the same time, Gage heard the slugs hitting their new target, then watched while she doubled over and cried out.

"Noooo!"

At that exact moment, chaos broke out from the front of the cabin as police sirens and the sounds of shooting resounded through the clear, cold air. That was quick. Must be these were the same state highway troopers he'd noticed earlier when they were closing the roads.

Just then the noise of helicopter rotors overhead caught Andrei's attention. Ducking his head, Andrei took a couple of hesitant steps toward his father's prone body but then stopped, swung around and disappeared past the corner of the cabin.

Gage was torn. Finish off the jerk or take cover with Elana?

There really was no choice. He put the Glock in his pocket and picked her up in his arms. It was only a matter of a few steps to cover, and as he knelt behind thick scrub he prayed for her life.

She lay silent and bloody, and as far as Gage could tell she'd been hit by two potentially fatal shots.

"Oh, God, Elana. Why'd you do it?"

As he cradled her, spoke to her, she made no sound at all and never opened her eyes. Her breathing was labored and her body was as limp as a rag doll in his arms. She was dying, and he knew it.

Gage couldn't believe what had happened. She'd taken the bullets meant for him.

But why? Why?

I love you, damnit. You must stay safe.

Her words, her pleas for his understanding, rattled around loud and true in his brain. She may have lied about many things, but the parts about loving him and trying to keep him safe weren't lies after all. And he'd never given her a chance.

Stunned and unable to focus, he stumbled to his feet still clutching her in his arms. He had to get her to a doctor. Nothing else mattered. And no one would stand in his way.

If she died now, he would never be able to tell her how sorry he was. Her past, her family, none of it mattered. He wanted the opportunity to say that he still loved her. Always had and always would.

Chapter 11

Elana's pain seemed almost manageable today. They'd moved her out of ICU just this morning, and the feeding tubes had come out in time for a liquid breakfast. But how many days had she been here?

The past hours, days, weeks or however long she'd been in this hospital had gone by in a blur of pain and medicine-induced comas. She vaguely remembered the doctor saying she'd nearly died. That her right lung had been hit and collapsed. And that she'd had emergency surgery to correct the damage done by another bullet that grazed her head.

She'd asked the nurses about Gage the moment she came to. But she didn't get an answer until the doctor arrived late last night when she'd been awake. He told her that Gage had survived the shootings and actually carried her out to the main road where a paramedic's helicopter could land to transport her to the hospital. He'd saved her life by not giving up.

The doctor also mentioned that Andrei and most of his Russian gang had been captured. Andrei's father had not made it out alive. The idea that she was finally free of the threat from the Russians hadn't really sunk in yet.

"How's the new room?" One of the nurses she was beginning to recognize came in with her cart full of testing and monitoring equipment—for the fourth time this morning.

"Have I landed in the never-ending monitoring room?"

The nurse chuckled. "It will be for today. Your first day out of ICU means we have to keep checking. But by tomorrow, things will calm down."

"How long have I been in the hospital?"

"Your chart says it's been five days today. It's Christmas day, you know. Hopefully you'll be going home soon. We'll see what the doctor has to say tomorrow. An early release would make a nice Christmas present."

"Uh...has anyone been to see me?"

"Not that I know of. Who were you expecting?"

Well, not her family, that was for sure. And she supposed Gage had gone back to Texas, too. It hurt thinking that he could save her life and still not love her enough to get past her lies and want them to make a life together. But as miserable as that made her, it might be for the best. Her father would never approve of a match with an outsider. Nor with the man who'd shot his boss.

Then it hit her. "My daughter. Gay, my little girl. She hasn't been here?"

The nurse shook her head. "I doubt the doctor would've let your daughter in to see you in ICU. That's pretty traumatic for anyone, especially a child visiting her mother. Maybe she'll come now that you're out."

Elana felt her pulse jump. Where was Gay? Still with Brendan? Gage couldn't possibly save her life and then take her child from her.

She endured the nurse's tests and then asked for a phone. The nurse told her it would take a little while to order one for the room. Then she left.

Elana never felt so all alone in her whole life. She wanted out of this place. Now. Today. She had to find her daughter.

It would be hard enough to go on through life without Gage's love now that she'd found him again. But to be deprived of her daughter's love, too, would be the worst thing imaginable.

Her eyes glazed over in a veil of unshed tears. She wouldn't be able to go on. Wouldn't want to take another breath.

With her mind and heart consumed with thoughts of her baby, she missed the door to her room opening.

"Hey. How're you feeling? Better?" Gage's warm voice washed over her as she turned to see him coming close.

But she couldn't speak. Was afraid this could be a dream.

"Think anyone would mind if I sat on the edge of the bed?" Gage smiled and eased a hip next to her. "I don't care about anyone else. Do *you* mind?"

She shook her head, too surprised to say anything. But when Gage took her hand, her voice returned with a vengeance.

"Where's Gay? What's happened to my daughter?"

"Calm down. She's fine. She'll be in to see you in a little while. I needed a few moments alone with you first. Okay?"

Breathing a sigh of relief, she finally looked up at his face. What she saw almost took her breath away. That same loving look she remembered so well was back in his sensual gray-blue eyes. It made her suddenly remember the bandages still around her head and that she probably looked like death warmed over after five days in the hospital.

But Gage didn't seem to notice. "You look better. The doctors promised me you would make it, but for a while I thought…" A lone tear escaped the corner of his eye as he swiftly wiped it away.

"You've been here? You came?"

"Of course." His voice was rough and he had to clear his throat. "They refused to let me in ICU, but I sat right outside watching you through the glass. Every day I sat and I prayed. It was touch and go for a bit. But you're a fighter."

"Gage, I…"

"No, my turn first. I love you. I have loved you since the very first moment I laid eyes on you. And I don't care what name you use or where you want to live. You're going to have a danged hard time shutting me out of your life ever again. I *will* follow you the next time. Right to the grave if I have to."

"Oh, Gage. I love you, too. No more hiding. And I want to be with you wherever you want to be. But my father. My family. Now that they know where I am, they'd never accept us."

Gage dropped her hand and swiped a palm across his mouth. "I have some very bad news for you. Are you strong enough to take it?"

Drawing in as much air as she could, she fisted her hands in the sheets and nodded her head. "Go ahead. What's happened?"

"Did you ever wonder how I ended up in Piñon Lake and spotted you?"

"Sure." Wondering what this had to do with her family, she put her questions aside and said, "I knew it couldn't have been a coincidence. How'd you find me?"

"I received an email telling me to look in Piñon Lake for someone lost. I thought the note was talking about my little sister, but that's not what it was about. Turns out that email came from your father. He wanted me to find you."

"My father? But how'd he know where I was? Why didn't he come for me himself?"

"Elana… Is it alright if I call you Elana? Alicia doesn't seem right anymore and I don't think I'll ever get used to saying Amara."

She nodded but wanted him to keep talking.

"Yeah? Okay. Well, it seems your father always knew where to find you. Even when you were living with me. Your cousin Brendan's wife kept him informed through the years. But your father knew better than to say anything to the Russians."

"All this time? He knew and he never said anything." She could barely comprehend what Gage was saying.

"I guess it was hard for him to keep the secret. He didn't even tell your mother. And it must've been especially difficult to hold his tongue when Gay came along. But Maeve sent pictures and let him know where you were. He wanted you to be safe, Elana. Remember that."

"Where is he now? And why'd he want you to find me?"

"He sent me that email when the Russians got wind you were still alive. He knew it would only be a matter of time before they found you, and he thought I could do a better job of protecting you and Gay than either the Keanes or you alone could do.

"And he was right," Gage muttered as his mouth turned down in a frown. "Despite what *you* thought. You needed my help to beat the mob."

Blinking back the rising panic she began to feel, she asked again, "Where is my father, Gage? Why isn't he here?"

He pursed his lips as though he couldn't—wouldn't—say the words. Finally he whispered, "Dimitri tortured him to find you, and your father didn't live through the punishment he received. I wish I could've thanked him. But…"

Her tears flowed freely. "Oh, my God. He…he…"

Gage cuddled her next to his chest and let her sob against him. "I know. I know." He spoke softly in her ear. "This news couldn't be more terrible. He was a hero for contacting me. But he wanted you to have an opportunity for a different kind of life. The kind of life you once had with me. Don't ever forget that."

"I won't." She fought against collapsing in her grief. She needed to keep going. Gay depended on her. And maybe…

"About what you were saying earlier. You think we could…um…start over? Have you given any thought to—?"

Gage kissed away her words, the most tender, most loving kiss he'd ever given her. "I haven't thought of anything else since the moment you were shot. The Russians are out of the picture. Their boss man is dead and your *fiancé* will be in jail for his whole miserable life. You say the word and nothing will stand between us. Not ever again."

At that moment the door opened and she could barely believe her eyes. Gay came skipping into the room with Elana's mother trailing silently behind her. Elana smiled at her mother, who tentatively smiled back. That's when she knew everything would be all right between them—eventually.

Gay, the too-smart kid, looked up at her own mother's bandaged head, then glanced toward her father, who was already holding her mom in his arms. And even a tiny little girl could've seen that all was right in her world, too.

She came to stand beside the bed next to Gage. "Up, Daddy. I want to see Mommy."

Elana gulped back surprise. "She's already calling you *Daddy?*"

Gage laughed as he lifted Gay up to the bed. "Don't try telling her any different. She's a tad determined."

"Stubborn, you mean."

But by then, the little girl who suddenly looked so much like her father was leaning against her mother's side and looking up at her with big tears in her eyes. "Mommy got hurt."

Gage gathered them both into his arms. "Don't worry, baby. We won't let Mommy get hurt again. We're a family now, and nothing can ever hurt us again as long as we're together."

Speechless and contented, Elana couldn't believe her luck. She'd been given a second chance.

And this time, she promised her dearest father in heaven, this time *no more lies*. She vowed to make it work with her Chance—now and forever.

* * * * *

COMING NEXT MONTH FROM
HARLEQUIN® ROMANTIC SUSPENSE™

Available December 18, 2012

#1735 COWBOY WITH A CAUSE • *Cowboy Café*
by Carla Cassidy

When rancher Adam Benson rents a room from the wheelchair-bound Melanie Brooks, it doesn't take long for passion to flare and danger to move in.

#1736 A WIDOW'S GUILTY SECRET
Vengeance in Texas • by Marie Ferrarella

A lonely widow with a newborn falls for the detective investigating her husband's murder and discovers she has some very ruthless enemies....

#1737 DEADLY SIGHT • *Code X*
by Cindy Dees

Sent to the National Radio Quiet Zone to investigate... *something*...Grayson and Sammie Jo find themselves fighting for their lives—and falling in love—in the midst of a dangerous conspiracy.

#1738 GUARDING THE PRINCESS • *Sahara Kings*
by Loreth Anne White

Opposites clash when gruff ex-mercenary Brandt Stryker sets out to save a glamorous princess from bloodthirsty bandits in the African bush.

REQUEST YOUR FREE BOOKS!
2 FREE NOVELS PLUS 2 FREE GIFTS!

ROMANTIC
SUSPENSE

Sparked by Danger, Fueled by Passion.

YES! Please send me 2 FREE Harlequin® Romantic Suspense novels and my 2 FREE gifts (gifts are worth about $10). After receiving them, if I don't wish to receive any more books, I can return the shipping statement marked "cancel." If I don't cancel, I will receive 4 brand-new novels every month and be billed just $4.49 per book in the U.S. or $5.24 per book in Canada. That's a saving of at least 14% off the cover price! It's quite a bargain! Shipping and handling is just 50¢ per book in the U.S. and 75¢ per book in Canada.* I understand that accepting the 2 free books and gifts places me under no obligation to buy anything. I can always return a shipment and cancel at any time. Even if I never buy another book, the two free books and gifts are mine to keep forever.

240/340 HDN FEFR

Name	(PLEASE PRINT)

Address	Apt. #

City	State/Prov.	Zip/Postal Code

Signature (if under 18, a parent or guardian must sign)

Mail to the **Reader Service:**
IN U.S.A.: P.O. Box 1867, Buffalo, NY 14240-1867
IN CANADA: P.O. Box 609, Fort Erie, Ontario L2A 5X3

Not valid for current subscribers to Harlequin Romantic Suspense books.

Want to try two free books from another line?
Call 1-800-873-8635 or visit www.ReaderService.com.

* Terms and prices subject to change without notice. Prices do not include applicable taxes. Sales tax applicable in N.Y. Canadian residents will be charged applicable taxes. Offer not valid in Quebec. This offer is limited to one order per household. All orders subject to credit approval. Credit or debit balances in a customer's account(s) may be offset by any other outstanding balance owed by or to the customer. Please allow 4 to 6 weeks for delivery. Offer available while quantities last.

Your Privacy—The Reader Service is committed to protecting your privacy. Our Privacy Policy is available online at www.ReaderService.com or upon request from the Reader Service.

We make a portion of our mailing list available to reputable third parties that offer products we believe may interest you. If you prefer that we not exchange your name with third parties, or if you wish to clarify or modify your communication preferences, please visit us at www.ReaderService.com/consumerschoice or write to us at Reader Service Preference Service, P.O. Box 9062, Buffalo, NY 14269. Include your complete name and address.

HRS11B

There was no way in hell he wanted the sheriff or any of the deputies seeing Melanie in her sexy blue nightgown. He found the white terry cloth robe just where she'd told him it would be and carried it back into her bedroom with him. He helped her into it and then wrapped his arms around her.

The idea that anyone would try to put their hands on her in an effort to harm her shot rage through him.

"I didn't do this to myself," she whispered.

He leaned back and looked at her in surprise. "It never crossed my mind that you did."

"Maybe somebody will think I'm just some poor crippled woman looking for attention, that I tore the screen off the window, left my wheelchair in the corner and then crawled into the closet and waited for you to come home." A new sob welled up and spilled from her lips.

"Melanie...stop," he protested.

She looked up at him with eyes that simmered with emotion. "Isn't that what you think? That I'm just a poor little cripple?"

"Never," he replied truthfully. "And you need to get that thought out of your head. We need to get you into the living room. The sheriff should be here anytime."

She swiped at the tears that had begun to fill her eyes once again. "Can you bring me my chair?"

He started for it and then halted in his tracks. "We need to leave it where it is. Maybe there are fingerprints on it that will let us know who was in here."

He walked back to where she sat on the bed and scooped her up in his arms. Once again, she wrapped her arms around his neck and leaned into him. For a moment he imagined that he could feel her heartbeat matching the rhythm of his own.

"It's going to be all right, Melanie," he promised. "I'm here and I'm going to make sure everything is all right." He just hoped it was a promise he could keep.

Will Melanie ride off into the sunset with her sexy new live-in cowboy? Or will a murderous lunatic, lurking just a breath away, add another victim to his tally? Find out what happens next in
COWBOY WITH A CAUSE

Available January 2013 only from Harlequin Romantic Suspense wherever books are sold.